His Highness Commands
PENDRAGON

His Highness Commands
PENDRAGON

Another swashbuckling adventure
for Victoria's Special Agent by

Robert Trevelyan

F
TRE
cop 1

Saturday Review Press | E. P. Dutton & Co., Inc.
New York

24489

Foreword

Bureau of Intelligence,
Home Office,
Whitehall,
LONDON.

9th October, 1856.

Sir,

Subject: *John Hawkdale Pendragon*

Your Royal Highness Prince Albert having expressed a desire for information regarding Captain John Hawkdale Pendragon, I have pleasure in making this report in fair detail for inclusion in your Royal Highness's own personal files.

He is presently twenty-six years old, having been born in the military fort of Rhotuck, India, in the year 1830, whilst his father was a serving officer with the 5th Bengal European Cavalry. He was returned to England for schooling in his ninth year, living with Sir Reginald and Lady Elizabeth Spence, his aunt and uncle, at their Hampshire estate, which he has now inherited. He attended Eton, and was later commissioned at the Royal Military College at Sandhurst. During this latter period his London home was the house of another aunt, Miss Georgina Carr. He has an apartment there at this time.

Captain Pendragon served four years with the 11th Hussars, firstly in their London barracks, and finally during their actions in the Crimean War. He led a troop of Hussars in the Light Brigade charge at Balaclava, receiving wounds as a result of which he was subsequently discharged the service.

He was appointed Queen's Agent a year ago, at the recommendation of Sir Sydney Herbert, and has proved himself worthy of the position. I take the liberty of reminding your Royal Highness of his brave and successful termination of the Russian plot of some months past, when I believe he received your personal congratulations.

He appears to have recovered almost completely from his Balaclava battle wounds; notwithstanding a slight limp, these in no way affect his capacity for action. As you will perhaps remember, he is a most presentable young man, of tall and virile appearance, and in much demand throughout London society.

I believe your Royal Highness's choice to be unquestionably the most suitable for the satisfactory conclusion of the present matter.

I have the honour to be your Royal Highness's obedient servant,

Page Cloverly
Director of Intelligence

His Highness Commands
PENDRAGON

1

PENDRAGON SLIPPED HIS HAND beneath his coat and took a firm
grip on the revolver. His palm was damp with a combination of
the light rain and the sweat of anticipation. The police outrider,
stern-faced and burly in his tight blue uniform, was now level
with him as he and Henry Cox stood waiting at the corner of
Piccadilly and the Regent Street Quadrant. The police outrider's face, shaved overclose between sidewhiskers and
moustache, gleamed. It was ten minutes to noon on Thursday
the 12th of October, 1856. For the two waiting men, seconds
had become hours.

Sixty yards behind the police outrider, whose sole job was to
clear the roadway ahead for the passage of the Royal entourage,
trotted the first line of troopers of the Household Cavalry. Three
fine young men, led by a boyish lieutenant carrying himself
stiffly, his sword drawn; plumed helmets and silver breastplates
glistened. Chained harness and equipment rang like fine bells.

"Smart turnout, Captain," hissed Henry Cox between his
teeth, his trained military eye critical but admiring. His topcoat
was turned up at the neck and he had pulled his flat cap forward.
His ginger hair was so close cropped and fair that a casual
observer would have guessed him bald beneath his headgear.

"The coach," Pendragon warned urgently. "On your toes,

7

Cox." He drew the Adams pistol slowly from his waistband, still keeping it concealed beneath his coat, and thumbed back the hammer.

The Berlin, its shining black sides displaying the Royal cipher, was thirty yards from them and approaching rapidly. The coachmen and postilions, in purple livery, watched ahead with official arrogance. The carriage drew nearer; matched grey horses highstepped in the fashionable style.

Pendragon could see Prince Albert clearly, the man's square Germanic face unemotional and barely smiling. He was leaning forward a little in his seat and nodding to those at the kerbside who doffed their hats, waved or curtseyed at his coach as he passed.

A barefooted street urchin, perhaps eight or nine years old and carrying a large basket of reeking herrings, forced his way cheekily between Cox and Pendragon. Cox reached down and pushed the boy to one side. The child swore at them, but edged away from the expected clip from Cox's hand.

The second line of State cavalry drew level. The coach was a bare ten yards away and followed by yet another half a dozen riders with pennanted lances.

"Now," shouted Pendragon. He had no time to watch Cox, but prayed the man was close beside him. At Pendragon's sudden and unexpected movement, the nearest cavalry horse swerved violently on the slippery cobbles, almost unseating its rider. The soldier's lance swung in a wide arc to clatter against the breastplate of another lancer. Pendragon reached the coach.

He grabbed at the polished gilt door handle and wrenched open the door. He saw Prince Albert only three feet away. The Prince's face showed no expression of fear, although instinctively he was pressing himself backwards against the leather upholstery. Pendragon swung his pistol upwards, aiming by instinct. He fired, and the explosion of the heavy charge deafened him within

8

the confines of the carriage. He thumbed the hammer and fired again. Behind, he could hear screams and shouts distantly, as though he stood at the end of a long empty cavern. He fired twice more.

Someone punched at the small of his back; hands grabbed at his shoulders, snatching at his clothing.

"Go, Sir," yelled Cox, his voice unnaturally high-pitched and wild.

Pendragon wrenched himself free of grasping hands. He caught a glimpse of Cox smashing his clenched fist into the face of a Lancer who had desperately thrown himself from his horse in an attempt to get his body between Pendragon and Prince Albert.

A studded boot kicked at Pendragon's legs, grazing him badly and bringing a bolt of pain hurtling up his thigh from its old wound. He managed to keep on his feet and force his way through the struggling crowd. After some yards it was easier, few people knowing for certain who had been the gunmen. There was a gap; he ducked his head and rammed himself through into the open street.

"You . . . heh! You there! Stop that man!" A Lancer swung his horse forward, spurring it to scatter the edge of the crowd and lowering his lance point determinedly as he did so. Pendragon sprinted away. Behind him he heard the clatter of steel-clad hooves on the cobbles. He jerked himself sideways. He caught a glimpse of a razor-edged lance head within inches of his face, and changed direction as the Lancer fought his mount, pulling it so viciously into a turn it almost sat back on the roadway. There were more shouts and screams. A thick-set man, by his clothing a brewer's carter, dived to try to grab Pendragon around the waist. He hit the man in the throat with the flat of his hand and swerved again. A small crowd in front of him parted fearfully as he waved the pistol in their direction.

The alley entrance, leading to the Saint Giles rookeries,

opened before him. A street vendor with a basket of fruit threw his wares at Pendragon's feet in a vain attempt to stop him, but Pendragon leapt over them, knocking aside a mad-eyed musician who still warbled a thin patriotic march on a tin flute, and was into the narrow passage.

He fought his way, still running, through the crowded alley. Behind him, the sounds of pursuit grew fainter. He ran, twisting between the packed and jostling humanity for another hundred yards before he dared slow his pace. Then, panting from the effort, he stopped in a narrow doorway and waited. Half a minute later, Henry Cox appeared, his face red and sweating, a long scratch down one cheek seeping droplets of blood. He had a swelling over one eye which was already colouring. He grinned as he saw Pendragon, and forced himself into the doorway next to him.

"We made it, by God Sir, but we made it!"

"And now, I wonder," Pendragon said grimly, "where it will lead us both?"

* * *

Had there been time for reflection, Pendragon would have thought it had all begun a lifetime ago. In fact it had started on his Hampshire estate but two days previously!

* * *

The wheat was yellow; a couple of weeks short of warm harvest ripeness. A light breeze playing across the sloping ten-acre field made it an ochre lake of gently sweeping waves. The horseman whom Pendragon had watched gallop the high ridge above the beech woods, took the thorn hedge optimistically, thrashing his animal wildly as it stumbled at a ditch.

"He be a ravin' lunatic," Crocker, the estate's old warrener, growled angrily. "That be good corn he's a-flattenin'. If'n Jake Foster catches he, there'll be a thunderin' murder, fast an . . ."

10

he paused, his eyes narrowing. "Over, Master John. Comin' from the right."

Pendragon swung his shotgun with casual ease, picking up the pigeon as it sped down the wind at some forty or fifty miles an hour. He let the barrel swing well ahead of the bird and fired. The pigeon crumpled in an explosion of grey feathers to arc down to the edge of the covert where the two men stood in the shadow of a lightning-split beech.

"Go fetch." Crocker spoke softly to his crossbred setter. The dog, with short legs and a long shaggy body, dived through the bracken undergrowth.

Pendragon handed Crocker the spent gun and took its freshly loaded twin from the old warrener. There was no need for him to check the priming; Crocker knew his job too well.

At the sound of the shot the horseman, now halfway across the wheat field, his horse chest-deep in the corn, reined fiercely and turned towards the two men, spurring his horse cruelly in the new direction.

When the man was some seventy yards from them, Crocker spoke again. "Blasted fool! Corn's due for cuttin' soon. That be one of they sailors from the telegraph. No wonder he treats corn so. Chances be the lout's drunk."

"Captain Pendragon?" The horseman shouted the question.

"Yes," called Pendragon curtly, angry at the interruption of his pleasure.

The rider galloped through the last fifty yards of corn and jerked his horse to a swerving halt only a few feet from Pendragon. He swung himself from the saddle so quickly that for a moment Pendragon thought the man was about to attack him. The man saluted, and wiped sweat and mud from his face with his sleeve. His horse, flecked with white foam, stamped nervously. "Captain Pendragon, I'm to fetch you urgently. You're required in London, Sir, this very day."

Pendragon stared at the sailor who, in his uniform, must have

11

felt as much out of place as he looked in the gentle Hampshire countryside. "I doubt if that's possible. It must be eleven already. By the time I've arranged my packing and informed my coachman it'll be mid-afternoon. The earliest I can reach London, even driving through the night, will be tomorrow morning. And I shall need good reason to go."

The sailor fidgeted uncomfortably and ran the back of his hand across his beard. "I'm to say, Sir, you are to waste not a moment, but are to take my horse and gallop fast as he'll take you to the telegraph post. There'll be another good mount awaiting you there, and another at every telegraph station between Four Marks and London. I'm to say, also, begging your pardon, Sir, you are to go straight to the residence of a Mister Cloverly . . ."

Pendragon interrupted him coldly. "And is there anything else you are to say, my man?"

The sailor's face deepened in colour, but he met Pendragon's eyes defiantly. "Yes, Sir. I'm ordered to say one more thing should you question me. His Highness Prince Albert commands you."

* * *

It was a hard ride, taken at a full gallop whenever the horses were fresh and the ground permitted. By six-thirty that day, Captain John Pendragon had collected his final mount from the telegraph station on the hill at Kingston-upon-Thames. As at every station before, a horse was saddled awaiting him; held by the bit ring, by a naval groom.

At Kingston, a grinning officer in a neat and well-pressed uniform shouted him an amused welcome. "Evening, Captain. You're setting something of a record, eh? A little over four hours for near on sixty miles! Damned well ridden, Sir."

Pendragon groaned as he swung himself from his exhausted

12

horse. His Balaclava wound had stiffened, making every jolt of the ride agonising. "I need a drink," he told the officer.

The man laughed. "A bath too, I'd suggest." He turned and picked up a leather jug from a table beside him. "We knew you'd need some sustenance, Captain Pendragon. Never let it be said the Navy doesn't extend its hospitality to the land forces. Here..."

Pendragon took the jug from the man and tilted it to his mouth. He'd expected water or wine; as it was, near raw spirit seared his mouth. He grimaced.

"Grog," explained the naval officer, his eyes twinkling at Pendragon's discomfort. "Rum and water. Courtesy of Her Royal Majesty."

"God bless her," gasped Pendragon. He lifted the jug again.

"Aye, there are plenty of sailors who'd say that on hard days." The officer reached for the table again and handed Pendragon a wet towel. Pendragon wiped it across his face. It smeared sepia with the mud of the journey. "Had I not been warned," said the officer, "I'd hardly judge you a cavalry gentleman, Captain. You look more like a ruffian poacher in that dress."

Pendragon's country tweed breeches were soaked with sweat, stained with green slime from the mouths of his horses, and covered with a patchwork of filth and dirt. He wiped the damp towel across the back of his neck, enjoying its coolness, and tossed it at the officer, making the man duck. The man chuckled and offered Pendragon the leather jug again. Pendragon shook his head and climbed wearily into the saddle of the fresh horse. He dug his heavy walking boots into the horse's side. "Thank you, Sir."

"God speed," called the naval officer. "Drop by again when you've more time. We've finer drinks at our dining tables. You're always welcome."

Pendragon cantered the horse along the narrow track on the rise of the hill. Far off to his right he could see the London

13

skyline with its eternal halo of industrial smoke. A few minutes later he was on the slopes of Wimbledon Common, and riding fast once more; he passed the sentries on guard at the gates to the military rifle ranges set to the London side of the tall windmill.

It had been a long time since he'd last ridden in this manner, almost three years; certainly three years since he and the men of the 11th Hussars, Prince Albert's Own, had made a five-day forced ride across the harsh terrain of the Crimea, on half-starved horses, and with inadequate supplies for the Hussars themselves. It had been a long ride then, and with no battle at the end of it. The men had been dispirited, sitting around meagre campfires, leaning against their saddles and honing the edges of their sabres with whetstones to razor sharpness; it was something Hussar troopers did when they were homesick or bored, and often a useful indication of the men's feelings. But, dear God, remembered Pendragon, there were precious few of those troopers alive now!

The regular thud of his horse's hooves on the hard earth of the road reminded him; the hoof beats had been just as even as this on his final active day with the Regiment. Unconsciously he urged his horse faster. Twenty minutes of fighting and his Hussar Regiment had been cut down to only two officers and eight mounted men. Balaclava! A damned ridiculous battle; a terrible waste of good men and fine animals. One hundred and twenty-five wounded survivors; hundreds of dead. For Captain John Hawkdale Pendragon a spell in the foul Scutari Hospital and his discharge as a result of his wounds; his discharge at almost the beginning of his military career! Thank God, he thought. Thank God for the kindness of his beautiful aunt Georgina, the hospitality of her household, and the skill of the London doctors. If it hadn't been for them, he would have been a permanent cripple like so many thousands of the Crimean soldiers now living in terrible poverty in London.

There was a shout ahead of him and the jangling of tin pots and pans brought him sharply back to reality. A small group of ragged tinkers leapt out of his way, their wares scattered, the men angrily shaking their fists and cursing him, the wives and children scurrying into the undergrowth at the roadside. He waved an apology and reined back his horse.

Below the common, the farmland was ringed with new dwelling houses that proclaimed London's futile efforts to absorb the rapidly increasing population attracted by the city's industries. The clean country air was already polluted with the acrid stink of sulphur from its coal fires. It was evening, with the sun setting behind the Thames Valley hills to Pendragon's left; the field workers were beginning their daily trudge home to their suppers.

From Wandsworth onwards the road surface was cobbled; the narrow red-bricked houses were packed tight enough together to obscure any sight of the market garden fields yet remaining within its boundaries. Groups stood in early clusters on the pavements outside the busy ale houses, men and women drinking to forget their squalid surroundings. Children played in the dung-filled gutters.

Pendragon found the river Thames and turned along the pot-holed road at its edge which would take him to Battersea Bridge. When he reached the bridge he swung across it, weaving between crowded and noisy traffic jams of costers' and traders' carts, returning, often three abreast, from their trade in the city.

Once across the Thames he rode along its north bank, skirted the high-walled penitentiary into Millbank Street and took the road leading beside the new houses of Parliament. By the time he reached Horse Guards Parade, adjoining Saint James's Park, his horse was stumbling with exhaustion and Pendragon doubted if it would stay on its feet for the final mile. It was with relief that he at last reached Berkeley Square. He trotted the tired animal into the mews beside Page Cloverly's house. Two coachmen standing next to an immaculately polished carriage looked at him, startled. A groom ran forward, peered, then touched his cap and took the reins of the horse.

"Captain Pendragon, Sir."

Pendragon slid from the saddle and stretched himself wearily.

The groom spoke again. "Mister Cloverly, Captain Pendragon, he's awaiting you, Sir, we heard you was due, Sir. They've been signalling your progress all the way, Sir."

"I should walk the horse a little," suggested Pendragon. "I think he's as tired as myself, but he'll chill from that muck sweat."

"I'll wrap him, Sir. And he'll get good mash of oats and ale."

Pendragon's legs felt as though they were about to collapse at the knees. His thigh wound was dead now, but he knew that once the numbness disappeared the pain would return and he would certainly have a restless and disturbed night. He stretched again, beat dust from his clothes, and limped around to the front of the house. The short climb up the steps pulled at his tired muscles. He raised the heavy brass knocker and let it fall by its own weight.

He had expected the door to be opened by Page Cloverly's butler, but it was Page himself who greeted him. "John! Good heavens boy, I'd hardly know you! A fine ride, John, barely six and a half hours. I doubt if it's been ridden faster. I'm sorry we couldn't give you more warning so you might have taken the railway."

Pendragon smiled wryly. It was true a railway trip might not have been as tiring, but even had Cloverly given him a full week's warning, it was unlikely he would have used a train with his own carriage and coachman still at the Hampshire estate. "No matter," he said. "What is so urgent as to snatch me straight from a bright day's shooting, without even the time to pack a saddle bag of provisions?"

"I prefer my guest to tell you himself." Page Cloverly led Pendragon to the study. He pushed the door open. A tall,

16

broad-shouldered but elegant man stood by the window, looking out on to the gaslit courtyard below. At the sound of the door, he turned to face them.

"Your Highness!" Pendragon was horrified to hear his words sound like an exclamation. He bowed, guiltily.

"Captain Pendragon." Prince Albert held out his hand. Pendragon took it and felt friendly warmth in the man's handshake. Prince Albert's eyes twinkled in the gaslight. "I trust you had a comfortable journey, Captain."

"Yes, Your Highness." Pendragon was standing at attention, and felt a growing self-consciousness at his filthy clothing.

"Why do my subjects always lie to me?" sighed Prince Albert, his Germanic accent clipping his words. "It is always particularly apparent with my army officers, especially those who have served with my own regiment. You all seem to think I am a child to be protected from anything that might cause me distress! Captain Pendragon, you have quite obviously *not* had a comfortable journey. By both the smell of perspiration, a bodily phenomenon with which I assure you I am quite familiar, and by the sight of your clothing, I perceive that it can only have been tedious and exhausting. Have you eaten, drunk or rested?"

"A mouthful of grog at Kingston, Sir."

"A mouthful of grog at Kingston," the Prince repeated. He turned to Page Cloverly. "Raise a bottle of claret, Cloverly. Better still, raise two." He turned back to Pendragon, lowered himself into a chair and indicated that Pendragon should sit opposite him. "I notice you still limp, Captain Pendragon. Does your wound hamper you much?"

Pendragon shook his head.

"Good," continued Prince Albert. "For in your official capacity as Her Majesty's Agent you may have need of all your strength in the days ahead." He paused as Page Cloverly's butler brought in a tray of wines and then waited until the man

17

had finished pouring glasses and left the room before he looked at Cloverly. "Check the door, please, we must not be overheard." When Page Cloverly returned to his side, the Prince leant forward in his seat so that he was but two feet away from Pendragon. "Captain," he said softly, "what you hear now is of a most secret nature. At this moment, only myself and Mister Cloverly have knowledge of the matter; you will be the third to share the knowledge, and I trust you will be guarded."

"Of course, Your Highness."

Prince Albert licked his lips. "I am not known as a coward," he said, his voice little more than a whisper, "though perhaps I would agree to eccentricity, if one can call riding to the hunt in what I hear rumoured you British sometimes call my fancy dress is eccentric. I am seldom fearful of the future unless it should hold a danger for my dear child . . ." he stopped, corrected himself, and continued, "Her Majesty the Queen. However, I have today received information of an attempt upon my life. No, wait," he held up his hand. "No need to interrupt me with a declaration of your willingness to protect me, Captain; I accept that as a fact, which I honour deeply. Captain Pendragon, this is no ordinary assassination attempt. I received a messenger this morning from Prussia. The special police of my Uncle Wilhelm have uncovered, quite accidentally, a plot aimed not only at my destruction, but at the destruction of peace within these isles, perhaps within all Europe. It seems a certain merchant, Gunter Albricht, had long been suspected of supplying arms to small groups of political fanatics whose present intentions seem to be to spread war throughout Europe; their purpose is the unification of the German States, as was that of the revolutionary army in 1848. Having failed and been outlawed for more peaceful methods, they have decided only a catastrophe on a wide European scale can further their cause." Prince Albert frowned and tightened his lips before continuing. "Prussian police are chosen by the Director of Prussian Intelligence, Herr Stieber, as much

18

for brawn and stature as they are for brains; they are not known for their human kindnesses to prisoners during interrogation. Albricht talked freely. He supplied all the names of the most important of the group's members, some of them statesmen's sons, men who are of a position to know better. However, during his interview, he gave one startling piece of information; I am to be killed."

"But for what possible reason, Your Highness?" asked Pendragon.

Prince Albert shook his head. "For what sensible reason, indeed? I, for one, would welcome a unified Germany, and I have no greater ambition than that one day it will come about by the free will of the Teutonic peoples. However, those of demagogic activity feel I have too much influence on the future of Germany, even from my position here in Britain. My old family relationships are viewed with suspicion. I am the husband of the Queen of the most powerful of European nations. I have apparent influence upon her and her subjects. The conspirators seem to believe that in the event of a German civil revolution I would be certain to persuade my wife to offer the services of her much respected regiments, for the protection of my many relatives, and of the various sovereignties within the German states."

Page Cloverly spoke quickly. "His Highness's death, they argue, can only assist their cause. It would successfully sever, perhaps permanently, any bonds between Germany and Great Britain. At worst, the assassination of a German Prince, if laid at Britain's door, might provoke such German anger as to bring an immediate declaration of war against Britain; which, too, could only serve their evil purposes."

"Surely the assassins will not proceed now they know their plans are in the hands of Prussian Intelligence?" asked Pendragon. "That knowledge alone must defeat them."

Prince Albert smiled grimly. "I fear that it does not. You see,

Captain, the assassin may not himself be a German. According to the late Herr Albricht, he is an international."

"An international?" The expression puzzled Pendragon.

Page Cloverly answered. "A current title, John, for those unwelcome in their own countries for their beliefs. Men such as Marx or Engels to whom we are so generous as to offer the shelter of our isle, and in which they have published their extraordinary manifesto."

"I am not so foolish to think I am a popular figure with all our subjects," Prince Albert admitted sadly. "You will remember the rumours of my imprisonment in the Tower, almost on the eve of the Crimean War, when I was suspected by many as being pro-Russian. It is not so long ago that Her Majesty was receiving daily requests for my internment. From these letters and deputations I learnt I am considered 'untrustworthy in the circumstances'—though God knows what circumstances they have in mind. I learn, too, I am thought 'Steif', overbearing, even humourless. There are some who believe my marriage to my beloved wife is nothing more than a cunning plot to take eventual control of Great Britain and even her empires. The worst doubt my plans for my eight children: I am founding a dynasty, they claim."

"Do we have a name for this assassin?" asked Pendragon, frowning.

Prince Albert shook his head. "Herr Albricht, unfortunately, expired before he could be induced to part with that information. Since the Federal Act, my uncle's police are often violently enthusiastic when dealing with those who disseminate novel political ideas." He spoke apologetically, as though because his background was German the matter had been his own responsibility. "We know only very little. We understand the man is sworn to the task, and that his payment is to be generous, a million German marks; which is considered, I am informed, a substantial donation to the man's own pack of wolves, wherever

20

they may be. That he will make his attempt is quite certain. He is, Herr Albricht said, a quite determined gentleman, one who kills not only for money but pleasure."

"A very honourable gentleman," grunted Pendragon.

"Let us not judge honour by our own standards," said Prince Albert. "Remember that a man-eating savage is considered honourable by fellow cannibals. However we do not know who he is, nor do we have any description of the man. We do not even know when he is planning to make his play. I have a greater personal worry; I believe it is not unlikely he may use some explosive device—they seem currently in favour at this time for the assassination of Royalty—and such a bomb, thrown at myself, could endanger the life of Her Majesty and my children. This is my greatest fear. I pray only for one thing at this moment, Captain Pendragon, that the man chooses to use a rifle, or a knife; with those weapons he is unlikely to make any mistakes. I cannot bear the thought of any threat of injury to my beloved family."

"Oh my God!" Page Cloverly whispered his exclamation.

"Is Her Majesty aware of all this?" asked Pendragon.

"No." Prince Albert smiled wryly. "She has problems enough, Captain; so many that at times it pays even me to keep out of her pathway. She is also with child, which tends to shorten her temper a little. No, she does not know of this matter, and I must ask you to keep her ignorant of it, at least for the present."

"Have we not the slightest indication of when the man may strike?" asked Page Cloverly.

Prince Albert shrugged wearily. "According to the information supplied by the late Herr Albricht, the man was given his commission a little over three weeks ago. He has had time to return to England. He will no doubt need a few days to make his plans; I believe we can expect the attempt sometime within the week or so at the most."

Pendragon whistled between his teeth.

The Prince leant back in his armchair and folded his arms. "Captain, I cannot order your success in this matter, as I might order a servant to lay out a fresh shirt. Nor do I insist that you accept what may be only a frustrating and impossible task. You are quite free to refuse me; it will in no way damage either your position, or our relationship."

"No task is completely impossible, Sir," said Pendragon softly. He hoped his statement was not too optimistic.

2

ONCE HIS HIGHNESS PRINCE ALBERT had left, Pendragon spent only a few more minutes in Page Cloverly's company before he too excused himself. He stood for a while at the bottom of the steps of the house and listened to the sounds of London. True, it was a dirty city, foul-smelling and a jumble of poverty to the east, but for Pendragon it was his real home and contained most of his friends. He stretched himself again, forcing movement back to his tired joints, and walked the half-mile to Georgina's house at 39 Park Lane. Although Pendragon was ill-dressed and still dirty with the grime of his journey, he attracted no special attention from people he passed on his route. In fact, he thought wryly, poorly dressed and shabby night wanderers were much less conspicuous than those in finery.

He took a route a few yards longer than was necessary, so that he would approach Georgina's house from its frontage opposite Hyde Park. When it came into view, he slowed his pace to enjoy the welcoming sight of the house; its white bow front and balcony were illuminated by the warm lights at the windows. His three-month absence in Hampshire gave even more satisfaction to his homecoming.

He knocked, and the door was opened immediately, as though Wolfgang, Georgina's butler, had been standing behind it in anticipation. He blinked, not recognising Pendragon for a second, then stepped forward as though he was about to clasp him in his arms, only to correct himself at the last instant and change the movement into one of respectful pleasure.

"Captain John, how unexpected! We are pleased you are back, Captain John." He stared at Pendragon's soiled clothing. "You have ridden, Captain John? We heard no horse in the yard."

Pendragon passed him his hat. "No horse with me, Wolfgang. I called first at Mister Cloverly's and left the animal there. It was exhausted."

"John . . ." His name was almost a shrill of delight. Georgina stood at the sitting-room door a few yards behind Wolfgang. She ran towards him, and hugged him. "Phew!" She pushed him away. "John, dear. You smell! Good heavens, you're filthy!" She laughed, looking and sounding a dozen years younger than her thirty-six.

"I've ridden from the estate today," explained Pendragon. "You look as lovely as ever, Georgina. I could stay away from you no longer."

"Tish! The thought of me has never dragged you from anywhere," she said, slipping her arm through his and taking him into the room. "The truth, John; why are you back so soon? You are not expected for another three weeks. I doubt Hampshire drove you away—not with your hunting, shooting and chasing of all the squire's pretty daughters." Her green eyes stared at him questioningly. She shook her white-blonde hair in mock anger. "Business, John. I know the look on your face. I wondered why Mister Cloverly excused himself from our meeting this afternoon; normally I have difficulty keeping him away from me." She pouted. "And what this time, John: Chinese with hatchets? Indians with cutlasses? Arabs with bowls of poison and hashish?"

He laughed at her. "Nothing so dangerous, Georgina. A small

24

routine matter. Look at me, I'm filthy, I should be in the kitchens. Forgive me for a while until I've bathed and changed, then we can talk."

"How unkind and thoughtless of me." She rang the servant's bell. It was answered by Henry Cox.

"Yes, Ma'am," he said, grinning a welcome at Pendragon.

"Look, Cox, whom we have home with us," Georgina exclaimed, waving her hand towards Pendragon. "As dirty as I've ever seen him. He tells me he prefers your company to mine. Perhaps you will see to a bath for him, and no doubt fresh clothing."

"Of course, Ma'am," said Cox. "Glad to see you back, Captain, Sir."

"And Cox," continued Georgina. "Ask Emma to see Captain John's bed has a warmer in it; it can't possibly be aired. And a fire lit in his room as well."

"Of course, Ma'am."

"As quickly as you can, Cox," said Pendragon. "I fear my fragrance pollutes the air."

* * *

Cox was standing in Pendragon's bedroom when, five minutes later, he climbed the stairs to the room. Cox was as military as ever, and no matter what civilian clothing he ever wore, it always had the look of a uniform. He snapped his heels to attention, as though his commanding officer had entered.

"Welcome, Captain. I heard from Wolfgang you'd arrived, and that you'd surely be needing plenty of hot water. The bath is full but scalding. I believe you had a hard day's ride, Sir."

"Indeed, Cox, but seven hours from Hampshire." Pendragon shrugged himself out of his dusty coat.

Cox spoke admiringly. "That was a good forced ride, Captain. May I suggest you relax before your bath, Sir, while it cools. I took the liberty of pouring you a brandy." Cox paused and

25

looked quizzically at Pendragon. "We weren't expecting you Captain. I hope it's nothing ill brings you back so urgently?"

"Ill news, yes." Pendragon picked up the brandy glass from the silver tray and moved to the warmth of the bedroom fire. He drank the brandy in one quick swig. Cox followed him and stood with Pendragon's coat over his arm. "Very ill news, Cox, of which I may speak to you later." At the sight of Cox's worried stare, he changed the tone of his voice. "No, not ill family news, Cox; just ill news. Not a death or a bankruptcy amongst us, but news I am certain will make you too feel uncomfortable."

"Yes, Captain," said Cox, now more curious than ever. He opened his mouth for a question, then thought better of it and took Pendragon's coat out to the laundry closet. He returned a few seconds later. "Another brandy, Captain?"

Pendragon nodded. "How goes it in London, Cox? Is all well enough here?"

"All's well, here, Captain, I'm relieved to report. Your Dasher is fit as a fiddle and hard as steel. Either Ted Blower or myself have been exercising him daily in the park. And young Ted, Captain, he has all the makings of a good cavalryman; I knew I was right on that first day we found him. He says he intends to sign on next year, and asks for a recommendation when the time comes. He's changed a lot; he can read and write now, and chooses his words a little better. I think he's a favourite with Miss Carr, for she likes him to accompany her carriage if she goes far from home."

"Has my aunt been keeping well?"

"As ever, Captain." Cox passed Pendragon the second glass of brandy. "I'd bet her as fit as Dasher, Captain, begging your pardon. And Mister Cloverly spends much time in her company. I hear it rumoured there might even be an announcement made by them soon. At least, that's what I hear from cook, who is friendly with Mister Cloverly's footman. Though, Captain, not that I place much strength in servants' gossip."

Pendragon chuckled. "Good for Page Cloverly if he leads her to church, says I, Cox. I like the man almost as much as I love my aunt, and I could wish neither of them better. Now be a good fellow and see about cooling my bath."

"Certainly, Captain, Sir." Cox turned to fetch cold water, then stopped as a sudden thought occurred to him. "Captain. This ill news; would it be of a nature involving you in government matters, such as the matter of last year when Rambolt the spycatcher was killed?"

"Of a nature not too dissimilar, certainly." Pendragon watched Cox's face. "Don't jump the gun yet, Cox, the time's not yet arrived for sharpening sabres."

"Course not, Captain, Sir." There was so little emotion showing on Cox's face, it was obvious he was controlling himself. Only a slight stiffening of his shoulders, as though he were flexing his muscles in anticipation of a fight, gave an indication of his secret pleasure.

"But," added Pendragon, "it might just be the time to take the sabres from storage and check they are still unrusted, Cox."

"I had a feeling it could be so, Captain," said Cox, softly. "Always been the same with me, Sir. I can smell an action a full week before it happens."

* * *

Pendragon stretched himself as much as was possible in the enamelled hip bath. He was as lean and stringy as ever; a fact which didn't surprise him in view of his recent inheritance of his late aunt Elizabeth's estate. It had been neglected both by her and his eccentric uncle for as long as Pendragon could remember. His three months' absence from London had only been the beginning of a vast amount of hard physical work, if the estate was ever to be fully restored and made profitable.

He rubbed at the long blue-tinged scar down his left thigh

and hung his foot over the end of the bath. The scar was painful to touch even now, nearly three years since the piece of Russian shrapnel had speared through his sabretache to embed itself in his leg, during the long charge. The tedious ride of the day had aggravated the wound. His legs were stiff and both calf muscles and the insides of his kneecaps had been rubbed raw by ill-made service saddles. Pendragon swilled warm water over them and rubbed them gently with the hard soap.

Now, in the comfort of his own room, it was easier to think about the problem Prince Albert had handed him. He still felt flattered by the Prince's choice. But, as Page Cloverly had pointed out once the Prince had left, it was the job of a Queen's Agent, and not the police, and as the Prince already had personal knowledge of Pendragon's ability he had been the natural choice; perhaps the only one.

Albricht! Damn the wretched man! And damn the Prussian Intelligence Service for killing him! Not that Pendragon felt any sympathy for those who were prepared to satisfy their vulpine cupidity at the expense of their countrymen's lives, but the man had died with too much left untold.

Pendragon concentrated, building together the knowledge he possessed of likely and dangerous subversive groups in England; there was little enough information available. There were the foreign espionage groups who appeared from time to time; there had been some trouble with Chinese triad groups, as he well knew, but after his skirmish with them, their activities seemed now to have been moved to the Americas where the triads were re-establishing themselves into gangs which the Americans called tongs. There were possible insurgent groups backed by Indians; their long grudge against the British Raj in India seemed likely to spill over at any time in the near future. And there were Marx's followers mentioned by Page Cloverly; so far, these had appeared to be no more than meetings where the ideas of Karl Marx and his friend Engels could be chewed over and discussed. There was little subversive about them at the moment in England. They met openly and in well-known public places and were, for the large part, students from the middle classes. Assassination was usually the work of the anarchists. Pendragon frowned. Anarchists recognised no international barrier or frontier, and seemed to recognise no authority either. It was known that groups of them, of mixed nationalities, existed in London; unlike the Marxists they kept themselves hidden amongst the criminal elements of the rookeries and ghettos. If recruits were needed for the discharge of any act that could lead to some national chaos, it was amongst the anarchists or criminals that they would most certainly be found.

"Blast!" Pendragon swore aloud. How much of a chance did he have of finding an un-named assassin amongst the millions of London's populace? The man might be of any nationality; he could be a common criminal working purely for money, or a misguided and ill-educated fool prepared to die for some obscure but dedicated cause. Where could he begin to look? How could he learn of a man whose name was unknown, whose identity was undiscovered, of whom there was no description, and who at this moment could be in any country in Europe?

Pendragon stood in the bath, and began towelling himself. There was no point in whipping up the horses before he knew the direction of the charge. Morning would be soon enough, when Cloverly had promised to have ready for him as much information as was available from Stieber. In the meantime he must wait, and be content with a mental picture of a man who was as yet only a ghost, but whose intentions were as terrifying and deadly as those of a man-eating tiger.

* * *

It was a heavy morning, with the sky leaden and the air warm and damp. Pendragon could smell London even as he shaved and dressed himself within his room. It was the smell of filth, indicating the early wind was from the east, carrying with it the scent of the open sewers, of industry growing within the city, and the foulness of the River Thames and its rotting banks where so much of the city's odorous effluent was carelessly emptied. So different, thought Pendragon, from the previous morning's soft perfume of his Hampshire estate. Twenty-four hours ago, he remembered, he had been dressing before a window overlooking sweeping fields of corn and hay, tall trees and rolling downland. Already it seemed an age away.

Usually he would have taken a light breakfast before exercising Dasher Charlie around Rotten Row in Hyde Park. Today he was still too stiff from the previous day's riding, and in any case too preoccupied with his new problem to consider wasting even half an hour.

He breakfasted hurriedly, before Georgina had awakened. He hardly noticed Cox's commentary on the state of the weather and the latest news of the city which Cox felt might be of interest to his lately arrived master. There was a welcoming note from Lady Zara Cashell, who must have learnt of his arrival by means of the servants' bush telegraph system, which was undeniably fast and certain, if sometimes inaccurate. One of Lady Zara's servants had delivered it only half an hour before, so it seemed likely that the news of his return must have reached her the previous night, perhaps through the good offices of another of Page Cloverly's household.

Zara's notes were infrequent, but whenever one arrived, it was invariably direct and to the point. This one simply said 'Call soon—Z'.

Beautiful and amorous as she might be, thought Pendragon, she must wait for his visit until this terrible business was behind him. Time was now too precious to be spent in her bedroom, however pleasant he might find the possibility after so long away from her.

Once he had finished his breakfast, he took his hat and cane and walked down Park Lane. He found a hansom a few yards along the road, its driver nodding away on his perch as he tried to catch up on sleep he had lost through a long night's cabbing within the always busy city. Pendragon attracted the driver's attention by rapping him awake with the knob of his cane against the polished side of the cab, then ordered him to take the shortest route to Page Cloverly's office at the Ministry's buildings in Whitehall. It was not yet nine o'clock, but Pendragon knew that by the time he reached his destination Cloverly would surely be at his desk; in his new post as Counter-Intelligence Chief Cloverly's hours were crowded and well-ordered.

On his arrival at the Ministry building, Pendragon was immediately recognised by Cloverly's secretary, who led the way up the winding staircase to the suite of offices on the second floor. Pendragon paused while the secretary knocked briefly, and followed the man into the room. As Pendragon had expected, Page Cloverly was working at his desk, his head down as he studied a sheaf of finely written documents. He raised his eyes as Pendragon entered, and smiled before waving the silent secretary from the room.

"I'm sorry, John; about last night, I mean." He took Pendragon's hand and shook it warmly. "You must have thought me an unwelcoming host, for I had no time to greet you correctly with such urgent business, and in the presence of the Prince. I'm glad to see you again. You look astoundingly fit and healthy for a wounded veteran."

"Veteran!" Pendragon laughed. "I always associate the word with retired soldiers of not less than sixty years of age; I hardly feel that, yet. And as for your apologies, they're unnecessary. I expected no more in the circumstances. In any case, I was so battered and tired I'd not have noticed had you tossed a bucket of ice water in my face." His voice became serious. "This business, can we discuss it here?"

31

"Of course." Page Cloverly waved his hand around the office. "No ears, as you can see. These rooms are made for private conference; the panelling is three inches thick, and set against Kentish brick. Even a shout would be unheard beyond the door. You can speak quite normally."

"Good. Then what have you that may give me some help in this matter?"

"Help? God willing, I could! Regrettably, I have very little of use to you." He indicated the papers on his desk. "I have these from Stieber, which report the interrogation of Herr Albricht. I spent the night here translating them in readiness for you. I know them almost by heart; have you ever read statements made under the pressure of torture? The Germans have much I admire, but their intelligence methods attack my conscience."

Pendragon took hold of the sheaf of papers. The writing was bold and positive. He flicked the pages; there were at least two dozen of them in Cloverly's careful hand. "A lot of hard work," he complimented him. "You must be very tired. May I sit and read them?"

Cloverly brushed his hand across his face in disgust at his own lack of manners. "My dear friend, forgive me, I get worse and worse. Of course, take a seat. Can I arrange a coffee for you while you read? Or would you prefer a glass of sherry?"

"Sherry, please." Pendragon lowered himself into one of the deep leather armchairs beside Cloverly's huge desk. He turned himself sideways so that the light from the wide window fell on the papers. Twenty minutes later he laid them down on the desk and took up the untouched sherry glass.

Page Cloverly looked at him questioningly. "Well?"

"Nothing," growled Pendragon, angrily. "Not a word to give me so much as an inkling of an identity. Not a description, nor a clue."

32

"Questioning only serves a useful purpose when the correct questions are asked." Cloverly banged his hand down on to the desk in an explosive movement of frustration. "Oh, we can't blame the interrogators too much. They obviously got *their* answers. They only needed to know the names of those connected with the arms smuggling, the hiding places, and the identity of those using them. They acted immediately and have all under lock and key; more likely executed, I would think. All but that man, Count Erik Von Oberstein, who we believe is extremely wealthy and the man financing the operation."

"The one they seem to have missed," mused Pendragon.

"Missed, but only briefly. They have his name; he is well-known. As we are both aware, John, once a conspirator's identity is revealed, or that of an agent, much of his power and usefulness is also gone."

"There's a description of him, as well."

"Quite. I believe we can discount him. To kill a King, that is what the confession says. That is the document's first statement relating to Prince Albert."

"Yes, King!" mused Pendragon. "Strange they should refer to him as King, although no doubt it is how he appears to them."

"I believe we are inclined to underestimate His Highness, ourselves," said Cloverly. "Remember, by now he might well have been King had it been only the choice of Her Majesty. She is much influenced by him. Damn me, and why not? She is in love with him and obviously so, and it is known her love is not only as a wife to her husband, but in many ways as though he were actually her father. It is quite reasonable she should be influenced by him. We are lucky he is a man of culture and intelligence, otherwise such personal influence would be bad for England."

"To the Germans, his influence must appear considerable." Pendragon tapped the edge of the desk with his fingernail.

"It *is* considerable," continued Cloverly. "I have no doubt, as he mentioned last evening, he actually *could* persuade Her Majesty to intervene in Germany's affairs, should he so choose. Oh, his danger to certain parties in Germany is quite real, and in no way imagined or exaggerated. From their point of view, he is far less dangerous dead, even at the risk of war. But remember, when this matter was first planned there was very little chance of his assassination being in any way connected with Germany or the German Empire. The assassin, even if caught, would be unlikely to talk. They will have chosen their man carefully for such important work. Why should we suspect foreign intervention?"

Pendragon drained his sherry glass and glanced at the papers again. "Here," he said. "This section. Albricht says, Wurter, Einbeck, Buchraeder and Von Oberstein. The names of the conspirators. It is here he first mentions the assassin." He paused and read silently for a moment, then continued. "A man, for a million marks; Horlm. That can't be an Englishman's name; what was the question they asked? Ah, who made the arrangement? Answer, Von Oberstein. Repeated question, who is the assassin? Answer, not known but perhaps Horlm. Question repeated several times, answer still unchanging. And was payment made in advance? No, but to be delivered by Erik Von Oberstein. When will the British king be killed? No answer the first time. Question repeated and the reply is, soon; very soon. Nothing more of use to us, Page, except the reasons, and we already know those. The questioning changes here and goes to another subject. Blast! Damn and blast! And the man is dead?"

"Quite definitely," said Page Cloverly. "I checked at once. It seems his heart just collapsed. A surgeon was present at the time and bled him, but he could not be revived. I have a copy of the surgeon's report, but it is of no use to us whatsoever."

"What of a bodyguard for the Prince?"

Cloverly laughed in a strained manner. "Bodyguard! Huh! You know the man; he is brave, sporting, and no coward. He totally refuses to use more than the usual bodyguards. He will not even carry a small pistol, though he is quite a respectable shot. Besides, as he pointed out last night, what can we do without upsetting Her Majesty? Anything obvious will distress the Queen, *and* it might be translated publicly as a form of open arrest—it could destroy him before the eyes of the British public, forever. Poor man, he tries hard to be accepted."

"I respect him," said Pendragon. "And I admit that I like him. Much of his gruffness and stiffness, I believe, is shyness. Still, if he refuses to be better protected there is little we can do, though I would have been happier with half a dozen officers from the 11th at his side. Damn me!" Pendragon thumped his fist against his knee. "Where's the solving of this problem? The man may be in London already, and planning his murderous action even now."

"I have been pressing for three years to have the Crown employees at the ports keep a record and check of those who come in and out of the country," groaned Page Cloverly. "The Customs and Excise men will have none of it. They claim they are overworked and undermanned as it is. Passage between countries, especially those who have been our past enemies and may yet be enemies again, is far too easy. A man may come and go as he pleases in Europe. Why, even children can be taken from London to Paris and sold into brothels without any knowledge of their passage! There is far too little control on our coastline."

"Even your proposed controls might not help in this case. No, Page, there's only one chance we have. We must put ourselves into the shoes of the murderers, and think as they think. We must plan an assassination ourselves, and see where that will lead us."

"No doubt to the deepest dungeon of the Tower of London."
Page Cloverly grimaced. "You are living up to your reputation,
John."

Pendragon stood and paced across the room, turning suddenly
to face Cloverly. "Look, man. If I planned to arrange an
assassination of, say, Prince Wilhelm of Prussia, then how do
you think it should be done?"

"You'd be as mad as he," said Cloverly. "I don't believe
you speak much German, and to the best of my knowledge
you've never visited the country. You know nothing of the
Prince's habits, or even pleasures. I doubt if you'd manage
it."

"Precisely," smiled Pendragon. "I wouldn't manage it. But
I don't think it would take me too long to find someone in
Prussia to do the job for me; providing, of course, that I was
both discreet and wealthy. Page, if I were to desire to assassinate
a Prussian Prince, I'd choose a Prussian to do the work for me.
And, if I were a Prussian, planning to kill a member of the
British Royal family, then I would hire the services of a British
assassin."

"An Englishman!" Cloverly seemed horrified. He frowned
angrily. "It makes the whole business even more distasteful, but
I suppose it is the sensible choice for them."

"And there is no English name amongst those given by
Albricht, before he died; only Horlm, which sounds Scandi-
navian. Therefore, Page, supposing my ideas are correct, then I
can also believe that even at this late stage of their plan perhaps
no such individual Englishman exists." Pendragon held up his
hand to prevent Cloverly interrupting him. "Oh, he exists all
right. But as a member of a group known to the German
plotters; as an individual who has, conceivably, not yet been
selected. I believe, also, that the selection of the assassin will be
the work of the English group rather than the Prussian."

"John, this is all supposition." Cloverly shook his head. "You may waste what little time we have chasing a non-existent stag."

"You heard the Prince's own words; it is all an impossibility. We have nothing to go on save a warning. Non-existent stag it may be, but I would rather chase a ghost than sit in Park Lane getting cramp in my backside and an ache in my head."

"All right, John," said Page Cloverly. "We'll assume everything you have said so far is accurate. What is the most likely link between those in Germany and an organisation over here? Crime? Perhaps! What else, then?"

"Almost certainly politics, or a lack of them," replied Pendragon. "Politics with an international link between them. There are few enough at that level. Politics and money—or desire of it."

"Marx's groups?" Cloverly asked.

Pendragon laughed. "Hardly, Page! Have you ever read Marx? Or his friend Engels? Well, I can assure you Marx sees no need for the kind of revolution which needs guns. He imagines our society will destroy itself, like a snake swallowing its tail." Pendragon laughed again. "Marx has provided almost endless subjects for debating societies. No, not Marx's Fellows. They pose no danger as yet, although I admit I have thought perhaps sometime, in the future, his ideas might crystallise within different minds to provide dangerous men with yet further motives for violence. No, Page, I think we can look amongst our own groups of anarchists."

"A single chance in a million!" Cloverly was unconvinced.

"No, not a chance in a million, Page. Perhaps a chance in a thousand. But surely any chance is better than none? I only need a hint, a single word; anything I can work on."

"Yes," agreed Page Cloverly, slowly. "Perhaps you're right. But I'd take my odds, rather than your own. Well, and where would you seek your anarchists?"

"London. Here, and nowhere else. Our assassin will be a man

37

who knows his way around our Metropolis. He will have his hiding places, and his friends. He will know where to buy illegal explosives, or special weapons. I suspect, too, that he will be a man of great confidence; a man who feels certain of his own escape. And he will be clever."

"And where will you seek this man within this city?"

"I believe I can make him search for me."

Page Cloverly looked puzzled.

Pendragon continued. "Anarchists and political assassins are strange men, Page. There are few enough of them, thank God. They seem to have a personal need for intrigue and death. Our political cartoonists are fond of showing them cloak-wrapped and clutching their bombs; the ideas are closer to the truth than the artistic creators think. I am of the opinion that to be an anarchist one needs an overdeveloped sense of the dramatic. One's ideas must always be larger than life. One must see one's own actions translated into heroic deeds of civilisation-shattering proportions. Hence their tendency to hide themselves amongst the criminal sections of communities where their stage whispers are easily translated into the shouts of modern Robin Hoods."

"And how do you intend to make your man search for you?"

"By planting in his mind the thought that what personal satisfaction he might gain from his planned action is already at risk. To give him the feeling an explorer might have, after fighting death and disease in a thousand miles of jungles, to find, within a mile of his ultimate goal, the deep footprint of another explorer who is yet ahead of him."

"How?"

Pendragon grinned. "By acting as an assassin myself. By publicly shooting Prince Albert."

"This is insanity," gasped Cloverly.

"As a Queen's Agent, I am a dealer in insanity. As you are, Page."

Page Cloverly was pale, and now angry. "John, your ideas are preposterous."

"Hear me out, Page, you've listened patiently enough so far. The scheme may be mad but it is the only scheme which promises a possible result. Imagine yourself to be our assassin. You are planning, very carefully and thoroughly, an attempt on our Prince's life in a few days' time. For the sake of your reputation within your organisation, and your ideals, and more importantly your own ego, you cannot afford any possible failure. Suddenly, out of the blue, someone else makes an attempt on the life of *your* victim . . . an unsuccessful attempt! How does this affect you, the assassin? For a start, your task is made more difficult; it is reasonable to expect a great increase in the number of bodyguards surrounding the victim, and far greater vigilance amongst them. The public are also aroused and probably many will be incensed by the action. Your chances of getting away are diminished. Also, and perhaps the greatest and most annoying factor, is that the unsuccessful attempt may well be laid at your own feet. People, friends, fellow anarchists, both here and in foreign parts, may think you a blunderer. If money has not yet been paid, it may be withheld; the offer may even be withdrawn. There is also the assassins' curiosity. Who is this man, or these men, who have made the unsuccessful attempt? Are they friends? Are they men with similar ideals? Are they perhaps rivals?" Pendragon paused. "I believe, Page, there are ample reasons for our would-be assassin to seek out the man who might frustrate him."

Page Cloverly walked across to the window, stood with his hands clasped behind his back, and stared silently for several minutes. At last, he turned and looked hard at Pendragon. "If there were any other way, John . . . if you were any other person." He appeared to relax slightly. "Suppose I consent to help you; suppose I try to get His Highness to agree, though the Devil

39

knows he will have every right to refuse. Suppose I do this, then I must know far more of your plans."

"I aim to end up inside the Saint Giles rookery in the Holy Land, a wanted man," said Pendragon. "The *most* wanted man in Great Britain."

"The Holy Land?" Cloverly was now even more horrified. The Holy Land was the warren of buildings running from Piccadilly, north towards Oxford Street. It was the haunt of criminals, murderers; every house linked by passages or overhead bridges; spikes driven into walls as foot and handholds. Not even the London police could enter. It was far more dangerous than the Bermondsey Venice of drains, or even an oriental casbah. Any criminal who entered the Holy Land might be safe from the police and the law, but his refuge could easily become his tomb. "You could not possibly survive, John. I cannot even imagine what dangers you could face once you are inside. Most likely your throat will be cut and you'll be fed to the sewer rats . . ."

"I'll survive," promised Pendragon grimly. "There is something in favour of my survival; a fast-earned reputation as a desperate and dangerous man. They may respect little in the rookery, but they bow to villany and force. They will expect both of me. To them I'll be as dangerous, and as unknown, as some wild beast. I will also be safe from the normal process of the law, and in the centre of the criminal grape-vine carrying information throughout the whole of the City of London. It ensures that I can be found by those who may choose to look for me, while remaining protected from any judicial action."

Cloverly snorted. "You survived Balaclava, so who am I to tell you that you cannot survive this action? You make a habit of making my prophesies look foolish, young John. All right, I'll agree, and help you. What will you need?"

Pendragon grinned again. "The Prince's permission. You

40

must persuade him, Page. I know from the Court Engagements in *The Times* that he is to visit the National Gallery tomorrow. Twenty-four hours is long enough for me to make any arrangements I need. Just ask him to alter the route slightly—by only a few hundred yards. Tell him I need him to travel in his carriage along Piccadilly towards Leicester Square. It's a fairly normal route for him and should raise no eyebrows. Somewhere near the junction of Piccadilly and the Regent Street Quadrant, I will make my spurious attempt on his life. I will be within two hundred yards of the alleyways leading into the Holy Land, and must take my chances."

Page Cloverly sighed. "John, my boy, you are almost certainly destroying yourself. Prince Albert may not be very heavily protected, but he is never without his outriders. They are all armed, our police are armed, and even respectable men in London carry pistols for their own protection. You could well be killed by any of them within a second of a threat to His Highness's person. He may not be the most popular of men, but many respect him and would protect him, just as you would yourself."

"It's another risk," shrugged Pendragon. "This whole business is a conglomeration of risks, but you must convince His Highness it is the only chance we have—however slim it may seem to him."

"And what after you have fired your shots? I assume you will load your pistol only with powder and wad."

Pendragon nodded. "A double charge of powder to make plenty of noise, but nothing in the barrel more dangerous than a stuffing of soft wax. As far as my plans after the shots; I will take to my heels and try to make the Holy Land. Once there, I can do little but hide, wait, and perhaps question."

"John Pendragon," said Page Cloverly, sadly. "I trust you have already made your will."

* * *

41

Cox's face was purple. "Shoot, Captain! The Prince? Damn me, Sir, you Sir!"

"And you too, Cox, should you be willing." Pendragon was chuckling at Cox's confusion.

"Stab me, Sir! Me, Sir?" Cox paused, stumbling for suitable words. "Well, Captain Sir, if you say so, Captain, but he always struck me as a reasonable man, and after all, he is the Queen's husband, even if he's German. No, Captain Sir, I'm sorry, Captain, but I've had second thoughts. It ain't right, begging your pardon, Captain, and even at the risk of you standing me off, I have to refuse, begging your pardon again, Sir."

Pendragon laughed aloud and Cox's face became even more puce-coloured. "Forgive me, Cox, for my villainy in teasing you. Like yourself, I'd die in defence of the Crown and the Crown's representatives. It was unfair of me to embarrass you."

"Joke, Captain, Sir," growled Cox, obviously feeling a little foolish. "Yes, I can see that now. It had to be a joke, Captain, didn't it? Very foolish of me not to laugh, Captain. Yes," his face brightened a little. "Quite a good joke, now I reflect a little."

Pendragon spent the next half hour explaining the German plot and his own plans to Henry Cox. Cox remained silent, listening carefully until Pendragon finished, then he stiffened himself. "I'm in, Captain Sir. Of course I'm in, God bless you, Captain. And there I was, thinking blimey, he's off his, begging your pardon, Captain, your rocker, Sir. But now, by thunder, Captain, Sir, I'll help you all I can. God Bless Her Majesty, Captain. God Bless her, and the Prince, too. But God help the pair of us!"

* * *

It was late afternoon when Page Cloverly called at Pendragon's home. Cox showed him into the living room, and took his overcoat and tall hat. Cloverly looked pale and harassed.

"Did he agree?" Pendragon asked anxiously. Cloverly's face gave no indication of the outcome of his interview with Prince Albert.

"It is my personal regret that he did," said Cloverly, pressing his hand against his forehead as though he had a hangover from a night's drinking. "I began hoping he would frown on the whole idea, but he is as enthusiastic as yourself. For two pins I think he would change places with you, John. He is secretly as madcap as yourself. He does fear one thing, however, that your attack on his person may cause an upset to Her Majesty's health, and so he has decided to give her a few brief details of your plan, a short while after the false assassination attempt takes place. He does not, however, intend to inform the Queen that there might be a real assassination. Just how he will avoid telling her the full truth, I do not know; she is an astute and probing woman."

"Thank God he agrees," breathed Pendragon with relief.

"He does not agree to your dying," added Cloverly. "I am to instruct you to act with extreme caution. You may be flattered to learn he values your life more than you do. And now, the times of his trip tomorrow. He expects to reach the National Gallery a little before noon. I walked back along the changed route on my way here; it takes a man on foot just twenty minutes to reach the corner of the Regent Street Quadrant, from the Gallery, so you may expect him any time after eleven-thirty. He will have the normal escort of twelve Lancers. There are two coachmen and two postilions. A police horseman will clear the route ahead of the cortege. His Lancers carry no pistols, only lances and swords. The police horseman, however, carries two saddle pistols. His postilions, although they may be wigged and liveried, are both expert pistol shots, and carry light handguns concealed in their jackets. There are also two muskets hidden in the coach's rear panels just above the postilions' handrails. A formidable armoury, John, especially since, as you instructed, his escorts are to remain uninformed that the attack is not genuine. I fear the risks are even greater than we imagined."

"Perhaps, but we have the advantage of surprise. I have brought Cox into my plan; he is quite trustworthy and I will need him once I am inside the rookeries. He speaks their language and learnt much of their ways in his childhood. And I know from past experience that he's a handy man to have beside you in a fight."

"Do you have all you need?" asked Cloverly.

Pendragon smiled. "As a two-man expeditionary force, we need surprising little; no stores, no reluctant packmules, not even a charger between us. A pistol apiece, money and different clothing. I have it all ready. Cox has purchased for me an admirable assassin's outfit. God knows to whom it belonged, but I suspect a poorish tradesman from its cut. It fits where it touches, and that's in few enough places. Cook has baked it in a hot oven for the past two hours to remove any possibility of live guests in its lining, though no doubt I'll find fresh ones soon enough."

* * *

It was dawn and raining when Henry Cox rapped on Pendragon's bedroom door. He entered a few seconds later with a tray of tea. Pendragon was already wide awake. He had slept well, as though the day ahead offered no more promise of danger than had those behind him. It was a trick which pleased him. Many times in the past he had awakened on a day of battle fully refreshed, when fellow officers had spent their nights either sleepless or in nightmare.

He arose and washed, but did not shave. Strangely, this change in his normal routine was more bothersome than dressing himself in the uncomfortable and shabby clothing which Henry Cox had provided. The shirt collar was at least two sizes large for him, and made his neck look thin and scraggy. He slid his feet into narrow black shoes that showed obvious signs of many cheap repairs, then stepped back and examined himself in the long mirror of his hunting wardrobe.

"Beggin' your pardon, Captain," said Cox, eyeing him with his head on one side, "but you looks terrible, Sir."

The man's seriousness made Pendragon chuckle. "But do I look correct?" he asked.

Cox walked around him, peering at him from head to foot. "Well, Sir, if I was to see you out, Sir, I'd never reckon you as a gentleman." Cox paused for a second, then sniffed. "Save for one thing; you smells too clean, Sir."

Pendragon laughed again. "And you, Cox, look a damned sight too stiff and tidy for a villain."

Cox looked hurt. "I'm not changed yet, Captain. I was saving it for nearer the time. Didn't want to go slouching around the kitchens being a disgrace to the household."

"The staff know nothing, I hope?" Pendragon asked.

Cox shook his head vigorously. "Not a thing, Sir. I've told them we're off on a caper to set a joke for some of your friends. I'm not sure cook agrees with it, Sir, but she believes me, I'm sure."

* * *

After breakfasting well, Pendragon spent some minutes carefully loading his revolver with powder and wadding. It was a good weapon, purchased only a few months previously from Westley Richards' gunshop in Bond Street. He dropped a handful of lead bullets, spare percussion caps, and the small pistol flask of powder, into his waistcoat pockets. His money was already stowed in the slim money belt beneath his clothing.

At nine-forty-five he rang for Henry Cox. The man arrived almost unrecognisable in shredded and tattered clothing. He wore no shirt, but appeared to have two dirty cotton vests on under his torn jacket. A filthy soft cap sat sideways on his head, and he had scrubbed coal dust into his face and hands until his skin resembled that of a beggar who had lived unwashed for half a year. His moustache, normally waxed, drooped untidily at its ends. His topcoat was tight across his shoulders and threatened to split as he moved.

"By God, Cox! Capital, man."

"If you say so, Captain," said Cox, sadly examining himself in Pendragon's mirror.

"Are you armed?"

"Pistol and skewer, er, knife," replied Cox.

"And who are you?" asked Pendragon.

"Henry Cox . . . deserter." Cox pronounced the word deserter as though it burnt its way past his lips. "Hired by you for a bit of dirty business, for ten shillings a day, and the promise of bounty at the end."

"Right, Cox, and what of myself?"

"I don't know you, do I, Captain? You've employed me for just a month or so. Where you're from, I've no idea, but I know you're a bloodthirsty and murderous man."

"Then don't use the title Captain, Cox," warned Pendragon. "Call me Mister, Sir, or anything you like, but no more of the Captain. Right, Cox, are we ready?"

"Yes, Mister." Cox looked around the room like a dog taking a last look at its home before being sold to a tinker. He gave a deep sigh and followed Pendragon downstairs, through the kitchens past two giggling maids and a horrified cook, whom he ignored, and out into the street.

* * *

The two men arrived at the junction of Piccadilly and the Regent Street Quadrant shortly after ten o'clock. The muddy pavements were already crowded with the usual hustle of London street tradesmen and their thronging customers. The roads were filled with horse carriages, hackney cabs, growlers and the horse omnibuses. The rain had slackened to fine drizzle and a distant break of blue across the clouds promised fine weather later in the morning. Underfoot the pavements squelched with soggy refuse, and the droppings of horses made the roadway a foul quagmire. A crossing sweeper at the junction forced his way swearing through the traffic, keeping a pathway reasonably clean for the pedestrians. Weather like this could double his daily takings from the grateful.

There was a line of shoe cleaners' stands along the edge of the pavement, their owners sitting dispirited on their boxes, with clay pipes jammed, bowls downwards, between their teeth. Rain was no good for shoe cleaning—a cleaned shoe was dirty again within five yards. They talked gruffly, swore and spat into the gutter in front of them. If the weather didn't clear by late afternoon they would need to beg the price of their night's lodgings and food.

For half an hour Pendragon and Cox stood in the shelter of one of the store doorways, behind the discontented shoe cleaners. Then the two men moved forward until they were standing in line with the others, at the edge of the pavement. Pendragon, his pistol jammed into his waistband, felt tense and keen with anticipation. It was all about to begin. The feeling inside him was the same he'd had on the morning of his last charge with the Hussars; a tautness within his ribs, an awareness of every individual muscle and nerve fibre in his body. It was as though the prospect of action made a man twice as alive.

Cox interrupted his thoughts. "The long alley over there, Mister, that's the nearest entrance to Holy Land. Will it be the one we use?"

Pendragon nodded. The entrance to the great rookery was well-known, he'd passed it a thousand times, but knowing its evil reputation had dismissed his curiosity. Soon, he hoped, he would learn a lot more of its mysteries.

"God!" swore Cox softly. "It'll be a long run. Almost three

47

hundred yards from . . ." He cut his sentence, realising Pendragon was watching something further down the road. He turned his head. In the distance, arms signalling at some obstruction hidden in the traffic, rode a blue clad figure. Behind him were a line of fluttering pennants on lance heads; the flash of blue and scarlet.

"Are you ready, Cox?" Pendragon's lips barely moved.

Cox nodded, slowly. "As ready as ever I'll be."

3

IT WAS OVER IN LESS than four minutes from the time
Pendragon made his first move towards the coach. Only four
minutes! Yet, as in any battle, it divided itself into seconds that
to memory seemed as many hours. Even now Pendragon could
still clearly recollect the startled look on the face of the nearest
Lancer; the droplets of rain on the polished handle of the carriage door, and the scent of rich leather that was immediately
masked by the overpowering fumes of spent gunpowder. Prince
Albert himself had seemed at first unsure, as though he
wondered if this was the true assassination, and then his recognition of Pendragon had brought an almost hidden wink of
approval as Pendragon fired the first of the shots towards the
carriage roof.

There were other brief memories; a flashing lance point,
startled faces; scattering people, and seemingly hundreds of
hands snatching in Pendragon's direction as he ran, twisting
and dodging, to the entrance of Holy Land.

It was over, and Pendragon and Cox stood together, breathless and a little shaky, some few hundred yards into the alley
leading to the centre of the infamous Saint Giles rookery.

They had attracted attention even amongst the Holy Land
inhabitants as they ran through from the entrance. The two men

now stood beside a heap of secondhand shoes, laid out for sale, above a narrow iron grating covering an entrance to one of the building's cellars. They were watched suspiciously by several curious urchins and the vendor of the shoes and his customers. The alley was crowded; people were coming and going to the rookeries; coarse tradesmen, rotting beggars in rags and tatters, and the overwhelming stench of poverty. The buildings themselves leant down on to the alley; old buildings, some yet timbered, with plaster falling away from crumbling brick and wattle. This part of London, thought Pendragon, needed another great fire.

"If yer want t'buy, look around the wares; an' if yer don't, then piss off," said the shoe tradesman. "I ain't got room for spectators."

A thick-set man, walking into the alley from the direction of Piccadilly, noticed Cox and Pendragon. " 'Ere," he shouted to anyone in general. "It's bleedin' them! Them as just potted German Al in his coach. Bloody murderin' bastards."

The group nearest Pendragon and Cox were startled and interested, unaware of the happenings of the past few minutes.

"They done bleedin' what?" slurred the shoe dealer. Gossip and slander were two of the few free entertainments in the lives of the inhabitants of Holy Land.

The thick-set man tried to excite the crowd, now gathering around him, to some sort of action. "A shootin', that's what," he yelled, making his voice even louder than ever and gesticulating wildly. "They done for poor Prince Al. Potted the sod." Feeling by now he was certain of some physical support, he made a grab at Henry Cox; it was a mistake!

Cox was far from as seedy as his strange clothing made him appear. Beneath his rags he was as muscular as an amateur athlete. His years of military training had taught him quick reactions. He ducked the man's hand, hunched fractionally, then drove his fist upwards into the man's solar plexus with so much strength that the man was lifted clean from his feet to crash backwards into the crowd.

The chance to rough-house was not to be missed, especially as it usually gave the quick-witted opportunity to steal something from the nearest stall affected by the fight.

A skinny youth, whose appearance belied his courage, or greed, launched himself in a dive over the shoe display at the two men. The dive ended when his head met Pendragon's knee, and he landed flat on his stomach on the neat rows of old shoes. The wares scattered into the crowd.

There was an angry shout from the shoe dealer as he tried to save his stock. A man at the front of the crowd, thinking the shoe dealer was attacking him, dealt the man a heavy blow on the head with a stick, and was immediately set upon by the shoe dealer's scrawny wife and two children.

The fight spread, instantaneously, even those at the rear of the crowd joining in, and fighting their neighbours. It was the moment for Pendragon and Cox to escape further into the Holy Land. They took to their heels and ran along the alley-way.

Some two or three hundred yards up it opened to twice its former width. There was a crowded ale house wedged into a corner of the miniscule square. Pendragon forced his way past a drinking man at the entrance; the man swung his jar of ale at Pendragon's head, but missed him, sloshing the liquid over another doorway drinker, who cursed in a dialect so thick with alcohol as to be completely unintelligible.

The bar was crowded, even at mid-day. Pendragon pushed forward until he felt safely lost amongst the inhabitants. The atmosphere was almost unbreathable; thick and pungent tobacco smoke, the scent of ale, urine, vomit and sweat. Pendragon's stomach heaved.

There was a jerking at his sleeve and he was relieved to find Cox beside him.

51

"God, Mister, what a stink. It makes my eyes water," Cox panted.

"We need a room, Cox. Will there be one here?"

"If not, they'll know of one." Cox eased himself sideways past Pendragon until he reached the bar. There was a girl, little more than twelve years old, serving the ale from a row of barrels; her face was no cleaner than the smoke-stained walls behind her that ran with brown condensation.

"Better let me ask," said Cox. "Begging your pardon, but with your accent, you'll be a bit conspicuous." He faced the girl over the bar counter. "Got any accommodation, girl?" Cox deliberately coarsened his own voice, so it was like that of a coster, roughened by shouting his wares in the streets.

The girl looked at him, her eyes sharp as an Earl's Court kestrel. She took in the state of his clothing, at an experienced glance. "You got any money, Mister?"

"Enough. We wants a room, girl . . . a private room."

"For 'ow long?" The girl never paused in her work, but began serving another half-drunken customer.

"Indefinite," rasped Cox. "Pay day to day." He saw the girl's eyes narrowing and added hastily, "In advance, girl, of course."

"Through the back." The girl spoke over her shoulder as she drew a jar of ale from one of the barrels. "When you goes out, there's a passage to yer right. First door is me Dad's. He's in there resting. He'll see to yer."

The door beyond the bar led into a dark corridor only two feet in width. It was completely unlit, and Cox had to feel his way along the wall until his fingers encountered a door recess. He hammered on it briskly. A second later the door was pulled open. The bar owner, built like one of his own barrels, peered out.

"Well? What yer want, then?" He was so fat his jowls quivered as he spoke.

"Girl said you might find us a private room."

"You'll be bleedin' lucky," growled the man. "What you think this is, the fuckin' Strand Spread Eagle? Eight to a room, I has, and them as is there thinks themselves lucky to have a sound roof over their 'eads. Threepence a night; in after midnight, not before. And out at six in the morning."

"That's no good, man." Cox turned away from the landlord.

"Wait. How much you willing to pay for a private room?" There had been something confident in Cox's attitude that warned the bar owner not to be too hasty in turning away the two men.

"Half a crown a day." Cox's tone suggested argument would be a waste of time, and an attempt at extortion might even be dangerous. "In and out as we damn well please."

"Rattle money then." The bar owner, taller than Cox, looked down at him. His chin made three fat folds on his neck.

Cox put a hand in his pocket and jingled some loose coins. "Right. Half a crown is reasonably satisfactory." The bar owner scratched himself under his heavy armpit. "Money in h'advance, see. Every morning, sharp at seven. First payment now."

Cox brought out a handful of coins and counted out two shillings and a sixpenny piece. He dropped them into the man's hand as though the bar owner had leprosy.

The bar owner was not slow to notice Cox's wealth, although the remaining silver was not more than a pound in value. But, where there was silver, might there not also be a gold coin or two? The attitude of the bar owner changed as he smelt extra profit. "It's a good room, cock. Dry as an old bone. Top of the 'ouse, so's it don't stink so." He reached into a back pocket and produced a stump of candle. He lit it, swearing as a blob of hot wax dropped on to the back of his hand. He led the two men further along the passage to a narrow staircase, then passed Pendragon the candle. "Up them," he said, pointing to the stairs. "Right up top. There's only one door. If you wants grub, you can get it in the bar." He lowered his voice slightly. "Course, if you wants female company, h'it's easy to arrange. Only no stray old slags, see. If you wants a bird, then wait 'til young Peggy's finished at the bar. She'll oblige you." He paused as the two men began climbing the stairs, then raised his voice. "She's all right is Peg. Got recommendations; good pair of knockers on 'er for a kid." By now Pendragon and Cox were out of sight, and a floor above him. His voice was a shout. "Well, then . . . no pissing out of the window! There's a bleedin' barrel on the landing; use that." He sighed, then belched. His tenants seldom bothered to make use of the barrel, anyway. He didn't know why he bothered to leave it there rotting; it could earn its keep better storing ale again.

* * *

The room hired to Pendragon and Cox was a garret on the fourth floor of the house. The only lighting in the place filtered through yellow waxed paper nailed over a broken skylight in the roof. The room itself was ten feet square; newspapers, pasted roughly to the walls, prevented damp plaster from breaking away. The floor was ill-fitting and of worm-eaten boarding, spongy with age and damp rot. There was a table in one corner, and a wooden slat bed in another, but apart from the two pieces of furniture and a few pieces of rags the room was bare.

Cox shook his head at the sight of it. "Eight in here! Damn me, Sir! Eight people in a room this size, and with no bedding except what they'll fetch themselves, and that'll be nothing but old paper for bed linen."

Pendragon eyed the squalid room. "We've little enough conscience about our poor, Cox," he agreed. "It does no harm for us to see this sort of a place now and again." He looked at the damp flooring. "We'll need bedding. A chair or two wouldn't go amiss. I had more furniture in my Crimea tent than's available here."

"Do you think we'll need wait here long, Sir?" asked Cox.

54

Pendragon frowned. "Perhaps too long, Cox. This may well be the worst part of the whole affair, just sitting in here waiting. Worse, we may be waiting to no avail; certainly we shall both feel frustrated. See what you can do about furnishings, we may as well make ourselves comfortable."

* * *

Cox had been gone over an hour. Pendragon sat on the low table, resting his back against the wall, mulling over the happenings of the past three days. It was like raking over spent coals; nothing fresh sparked to life. As he had warned Cox, it was indeed frustrating.

There were sounds on the staircase beyond the door. At first, Pendragon believed it to be Cox returning with whatever furnishings he had been able to purchase, but mutterings indicated more than one man. Pendragon slipped his hand beneath his jacket and gripped his reloaded pistol. The mutterings, seemingly in some sort of argument, reached the doorway. There was silence for a few seconds, then the door was pushed roughly open. The landlord, with two scruffy characters at his shoulders, stood in the doorway,

It took the bar owner some seconds before his eyes adjusted to the dim light of the room. He saw Pendragon standing silently in the corner. "Here," he said. "I want a look at you, cock, and the bloke what's with yer." He peered into the room. "Where is he, then?"

"Gone for the bedding and furniture you fail to supply, Sir," replied Pendragon. He slid a finger into the trigger guard of the pistol.

"That's him," said one of the men from behind the landlord. "I thought he come in this gaff. I was bloody sure, like I told yer."

"Him?" asked the landlord.

The second of the two men spoke. His voice was a bronchial

wheeze. "Yeah, that's the geezer. He was with a short ginger-nobbed bloke. I saw 'em clear as a diamond, the murderin' pair of 'em."

"You'd be best comin' with us, mate," said the first man to Pendragon. His voice was a threat. "There's a shout out for you, and an hefty one at that. A bleeding hue and cry. An' come quiet like for your own good."

The bar owner turned on the man, angrily. "Just you lay it, cockie," he warned him. "This man's paid his lodging, all fair and square. He don't have to go *no* place as far as I'm concerned. You know my reputation; I don't give no one to no one as long as they ain't bothered me. I don't care what he's done, no more'n you does. There's plenty worse in the rookeries, and you're no damn better. If you think you'll take him for the crushers for a little gold, then you've another think coming. Big Ted don't hold wiv selling a man for gold; no more do Big Ted's mates. Now push off, the pair of you, before I do you."

The first of the two men opened his mouth to argue, but the landlord spun him by the shoulder and barged him violently out of the door. "Away, I said. You know bloody better than to argue with me. Out before I smash your heads." He waited while the two men grumbled their way down the stairs, then he turned to Pendragon. "Well, the bastards! They'd sell their grandmothers for a shant of beer. You . . . don't think I'm happy with you neither. If I'd known what you was at, before I took your silver, I'd have had you on the street as well. But a bargain's a bargain, though why I'd risk my neck for your half crown a day, I don't know."

"I'm grateful." Pendragon relaxed. He took his hand from his pistol.

"Filthy ponces," growled the landlord. "They make me sick. They wanted you for a miserly reward. Oh, don't think I'm not fond of gold; I'm as fond as the next man, only I don't happen to have any love for the police. I've a son in Australia 'cus of

56

them bastards; for playing three walnut shells on London Bridge—what a crime, damn them! I cons what you've done, and I don't particularly hold with it. God knows what you did it for; I don't see profit in that action. But as long as you stay in this bar, none'll take you. If you step in a street, then remember you're as likely worth more money dead than alive . . . to anyone! "

* * *

That Henry Cox was finding his present situation traumatic was obvious on his return from the shopping trip. He pushed the door closed behind him, tossed a heavy bundle of mattresses and blankets to the floor, and leant back against a wall as though exhausted.

He pulled a handkerchief from a pocket and wiped it across his sweating face. "Blimey, Captain. We've really loosed a pike in the carp pond. There's talk about us everywhere; talk of a reward of fifty thousand pounds. Not that we should believe it, for there's no doubt the size of the bounty increases with every mouth that passes the news."

"It was to be expected." Pendragon remained outwardly calm; Cox's anxiety was quite enough without him reinforcing it with his own. Secretly, however, he found the thought of the mobs of the Holy Land, encouraged to action by even the rumour of such a vast reward for their capture, was making the fine hairs on the back of his neck tingle. "What else did you learn?"

"Learn, Captain?" Cox, normally imperturbable, widened his eyes. "I heard one group of villains saying they should seek us out and hang us before passing us to the runners. Talking about themselves as law-abiding citizens, though I'd swear there was none present who'd ever earnt an honest crust. It's amazing how the thought of reward can make a rogue virtuous. I think we'll be lucky to survive this night."

Pendragon said nothing. There was no reason to doubt Cox's assessment, the man had been a soldier too long to exaggerate danger. The situation had become more hazardous than Pendragon had expected. The plan had always contained elements of considerable peril, even though he had underestimated the reaction of the inhabitants of the rookeries. It was quite clear, however, that he must severely limit the time the pair of them could spend in the Holy Land. Already some of the rogues of the area knew their whereabouts; it would be only a matter of hours before they drew together into a gang to capture them. The landlord had voiced his feelings strongly to the men who had visited and identified Pendragon earlier, but it was most unlikely he would risk his life and property if it came to defending his guests against even a small mob. Though it meant the failure of his plan, Pendragon realised he must leave the Holy Land before dawn. It would be suicide to remain longer. The possibility of success had diminished. Soon it would simply be a matter of his own, and Cox's, survival. As each minute passed the personal danger increased; there would be a point beyond which it was certain death to continue. It was like trying to defend an insecurable position while countless enemy forces of far superior strength set themselves out in battle array all around. The difficulty would be in judging the final moments when escape was still possible; perhaps it was already too late.

Pendragon forced his brief indecision aside. Battles had been lost in the past by just such feelings. History had shown that determination and courage could pay fine dividends; and this situation, in many ways, was another battle. The skill now would be in deciding when the chance of success was completely past, and bravery had become foolishness.

* * *

It was after midnight, and Pendragon slept fitfully. Cox was awake, taking a turn at keeping guard, and passing the time by

58

hunting bed bugs on the walls with the flame of a candle. There were hundreds of them, and Cox's problem was not seeking them out, but deciding which of the blood-sucking parasites he would exterminate next. He intended to fumigate the room with sulphur candles the next day, and regretted not thinking about them before when he'd purchased the bedding.

There was only the slightest sound outside the garret door, but Cox's keen ears picked it up. With a movement as silent as a fox stalking a hare, he put the candle on the floor and moved across the room. He shook Pendragon, but he too was awake, his pistol already in his hands. Pendragon jerked his head in the direction of the door and Cox moved again to station himself beside it. They expected a sudden burst of movement; the door, perhaps, to be smashed off its hinges. Instead, there was a soft tapping, as someone on the outside rattled their fingernails against the woodwork in a gentle signal.

"Open it," hissed Pendragon. He pushed himself up, and stood to the side of Cox, his pistol ready. Cox slid back the newly fitted bolt and inched the door open, carefully.

A voice, little louder than the caller's tapping, whispered from the darkness. "Sirs?"

"There's a pistol at your head," warned Pendragon. "Step forward slowly."

A small figure moved into the candlelight. It was the girl who had been serving in the bar, the landlord's daughter. Her eyes were wide as she looked around her.

"Are you alone, girl?" asked Cox.

The girl nodded her head. She spoke again, her voice warbling with nervousness. "I'm sent to speak with you."

Pendragon pushed the door closed behind her and slid the bolt. The click of metal made the girl jump, startled. She was slightly built, not even five feet tall, and so thin that her cheeks sank inwards, prematurely ageing her features. If, as the bar owner had suggested, she had good breasts for her age, they were

59

well hidden beneath a shapeless and grubby linen dress reaching to her ankles.

"I'm Peg, Sir. From the bar."

"We know who you are, and it's late for visiting, girl," growled Cox. "There's no business for you up here."

The girl seemed less afraid now. She chirruped, cheekily. "Me last customer's only just gone, see. I was set to clean the bar; it's me work, or else I gets beaten. An' don't think I'm 'ere to please you, 'cus I has to be asked, nicely." She made a show of examining Cox. "Don't know as how I'd care for the likes of you, Mister. A girl has her fancies, and you ain't one of mine."

"What do you want, Peg?" asked Pendragon. The girl had noticed his pistol and was staring at it. Her nervousness returned and she shivered. He slipped the pistol into his pocket and indicated that Cox should do likewise.

"A man, Mister," said the girl. "Down in the bar. He was sat so quiet and still when I closed the doors, I never seen 'im; not until I fetched me broom, that is. Sat there like a ghost. Fair made me jump out of me skin, he did. He said there was two men here he'd want to see. I says, no there ain't. An' he said oh yes there was and he knew they was dossing here. He swears to God he means no harm and give me this." The girl held out her hand and a silver coin shone dully.

Pendragon looked briefly at Cox, then at the girl again.

The girl dropped her eyes. "I knows what you two done," she said. "Most everybody does. There's been a lot of talk in the bar; talk of a police reward, too, and many would turn you over for it. Me Dad and me wouldn't, it's a promise, misters; not since they took our Fred."

Pendragon softened his voice. "This man, Peg, downstairs, do you think him a police agent or a spy?"

"No, he ain't them; not neither," said the girl, firmly and with no hesitation. "I can spot a crusher an 'undred feet away. I'd say this geezer was in service, though a low kind, I'd guess. Not

60

in service with a gentleman but perhaps for a tradesman. Cor, an' he don't half smell of cats! "

"And did he threaten you?"

"Oh no. Should he a done that, I'd have raised a cry to warn me Dad. No, he was fair polite, but by the way he spoke he pressed me. He promised he wants only a meeting and nought else." The girl showed the money again. "I don't see too many silver crowns of my own." She looked anxiously at Pendragon. "I ain't sold you, Mister, honest I ain't. If I'd guessed he meant harm, a broken jaw wouldn't have got me to lead him to you."

"Well, Sir?" asked Cox.

"We'll see him," replied Pendragon. "I suspect he may be just the man I want to meet. Or, at least, the first step towards him."

* * *

The gaslights in the bar still hissed as the girl led them through the doorway. The bar itself smelt only fractionally better than it had when Pendragon first entered and it was full of its drunken customers. The floor was a swamp of spilt beer and debris; two sacks of fresh sawdust stood near the door, ready to recoat the stone flags. A man stood against the bar, his back to Pendragon and Cox. His clothing was coarse, of the kind of cloth Pendragon would expect in a pair of gamekeeper's breeches. The cut of his suit, however, as the girl had said, was more that of a tradesman's servant.

The man glanced sideways as the door creaked.

"Move slowly, my lad," Cox warned him.

The man kept his hands in sight at waist level, and eased himself round to face them. He was extremely powerfully built, with enormous thick-set shoulders, bull-neck, and the face of a prize fighter.

"Well?" asked Pendragon.

The man stared at them as though they failed to fit into the pattern he had already built in his mind. "There was a little funny business near the Quadrant this morning. Might you two be those gentlemen concerned?"

"We might be," said Pendragon, cautiously.

"As you have your hand in your pocket, Sir, I'd suspect it to be holding a pistol. Let me see it." The man's tone was confident and showed no fear at the possible danger of his request.

Pendragon, a little startled by the man's coolness, brought out the pistol, slowly. He kept it aimed at the man's broad chest.

"A revolver!" The man snorted with satisfaction. "If it'd been a single shot pocket-murderer, I'd have thought you a liar; it was a revolver used on the job, you see, gentlemen, and that was what I wanted. No need to keep it aimed, Sir, you've no cause to fear me."

"And who exactly are you?" Pendragon asked.

The man smiled; smiled or sneered, it was hard to decide. His nose had been broken several times, and his lips were thickened. "Who, exactly? Why, Sir, even my mother wouldn't be able to answer that! What exactly, is far easier. For some purposes, I'm a messenger. For my own, I'm a number of things; some could say valet, others companion. My employer might call me bodyguard. I've no God, so a Minister would name me heathen. I may even be death himself; or the pilgrim, Salvation. Make your choice. My name is Cragg."

Cox looked puzzled at Pendragon.

Pendragon motioned the man toward a table. "Sit, Mister Cragg, but keep your hands where I can see them." The man moved, sat on one of the benches and placed his hands, palm downwards, on the table. Now he was closer the smell of animals and sweat was almost overpowering. No wonder the girl had commented! Pendragon avoided the temptation to hold a handkerchief to his nose and sat opposite the man, his pistol ready and aimed at the man's head. Cox stood a few feet away, watching carefully. "And now, Mister Cragg," said Pendragon, "I think you'd better tell us what you want."

Cragg sniffed, cleared his throat, and spat into the filthy sawdust on the bar floor. He wiped the back of his hand across his mouth. "Your company, Sirs. I'm sent to offer you better board and lodging than you find around here. And better safety, too. If you rest here, then sure as the Tyburn gallows is oak you'll be dead or handed to chains within twenty-four hours. You're marked men. There's talk of a thousand guinea reward, and if that's guaranteed, there's scarcely a weasel within these infested galleries who wouldn't skin you for a hundredth of it. You may think there's none who know your faces, but I heard boasts from several in 'ere tonight who claim they'd recognise you."

"And where would you take us?" Pendragon watched the man's face.

Cragg chuckled. "For your safety, and my own, I'd not disclose that at this minute. You think not to trust me? If I'd decided you dead, Sirs, you'd be bleeding on the floor now. You don't believe me? Then look at this." The man ignored Pendragon's pistol, still pointing at him across the table, and jerked open his top coat. A thick black square of leather and metal plate was strapped across his chest. In its centre was a strange weapon, a pistol with a barrel no longer than half an inch, and with its firing mechanism built on to the heavy pad of hide. The man chuckled again. "A French patent, Sirs. Fires by a cord through my sleeves . . . short range, but loaded with five balls of buck shot. Kills at three yards. There's another at my back, too. I have further pistols in both topcoat pockets. You'd have needed a clean shot between my eyes to stop me, and even then, if my arms dropped suddenly, as like as not this little device would nail you. No, gentlemen, if I'd wanted you dead, then dead you'd be by now. As for taking you by force, then a shilling a man would buy me an army here in Holy Land. I could have you trussed, packaged and delivered if I so decided."

"I think we have little choice but to go with you," said Pendragon, controlling his voice so no sign of his excitement showed.

"Absolutely no choice whatsoever, Sirs," replied Cragg calmly.

* * *

At first Pendragon believed their destination to be within the Holy Land itself, for Cragg led them north through its centre. It was a maze of alleys and passageways and Pendragon realised that, even if he changed his mind and decided to leave Cragg, there was no chance of him now finding his own way back to the ale house. There were still a few figures moving around in the narrow passages, and heaps of rags at the sides of the buildings served as beds for the unfortunates who could not scratch even a penny for the cheapest doss. The alleys and passages were, however, unlit except for the odd patches of pale light that shone from unglazed windows.

Cragg chose his route without hesitation; he was completely familiar with his surroundings. After a ten-minute walk at a pace which made Pendragon perspire, the man paused. They stood in what, at first sight, appeared to be only a narrow path between walls of tumbledown rubble, which threatened to collapse should the men be careless enough to touch them.

"Watch your steps," warned their guide, picking his way over a heap of crumbling bricks. A fallen beam lay across his path, but he stooped beneath it. It hid a doorway so narrow that his broad-shouldered body hid it from sight until he ducked inside.

Pendragon tensed, wondering if this was their destination at last, or whether he might expect a sudden ambush from within. He followed the man. A few feet beyond the doorway the man stopped again. There was the flare of a match and he lit a small pocket bull's-eye lamp. Its rays shone down a filthy passage.

The man continued on for another thirty yards, then led the way down a flight of stone steps into an old and disused dry sewer. There were men and women sleeping, in indescribable filth, on the curving brickwork floor; they moved restlessly as the light disturbed them. Pendragon noticed rats scurrying in and out of one of the moving heaps of clothing, and shuddered at the thought of the condition of the human being hidden inside.

Another hundred yards along the foul passage Cragg climbed four iron rungs set into the wall, and crawled into an even narrower tunnel that at some time must have been a service sewer to the larger one. After fifty more feet he stopped. The passage was blocked by a heavy oak door shaped and constructed like the end of a large port cask. Cragg banged on it sharply, in a pattern that was obviously a signal. After a few seconds he rapped again. There was the sound of several bolts being drawn and the door moved.

"Jack Ketch's damned eyeballs," said Cragg. The words were nonsense to Pendragon, but satisfied the doorkeeper. A chain rattled free and the oak door swung open.

"Christ!" complained a voice. "A bleeder don't get any rest of a night on this watch."

"And nor you should," grunted Cragg. "You're paid to guard this shutter. There are three of us to pass. Look lively."

"All right . . . all right . . ." moaned the voice. "Come through. And be sure you all clean yourselves up before you pass beyond the next room."

Pendragon and Cox followed Cragg through the small circular doorway. Behind them the door slammed closed and the bolts were shot back into place. "Wait," said the voice. A gaslight on the wall was turned up, to illuminate the room brightly and force the men to shield their eyes. Pendragon's guide blew out the flame of his bull's-eye lamp, waited a few seconds until it had cooled and slipped it into his pocket.

The room was a cellar, and most of its walls were lined with wine barrels. Looking behind him at the wall from where they had emerged, Pendragon was surprised to find he could not identify the entrance to the passage. It was obviously one of the stacked barrels, but which he wasn't sure.

The man who had been guarding the door was slightly hunch-backed, shrunken and wizened. He pointed across the room. "There's a water pail there, and a cloth. Clean and tidy your-selves if needs be. A brush there will get dust from your clothing."

It took the men a few minutes to rid themselves of the grime of their journey. When they were ready the hunch-back inspected them. "Pretty poor, but perhaps you'll pass," he said. He walked to an iron ladder and clambered up, pausing to slide a cover away at the top. He peered out, then returned down the rusty steps. "It's clear. You know the way?"

"I know." Cragg pulled himself up the ladder, paused, and signalled Cox and Pendragon to follow him. When they stood beside him on the landing above, he slid the cover back across the cellar entrance and kicked a carpet over it. "This is a brothel, so don't be surprised at any noises you may hear. Just follow me, cool like, as though we're friends who've been enjoying ourselves and are on our ways home. You're clear of Holy Land now. This is the secret entrance. Well hidden, for not many know its whereabouts; certainly not the law."

He led them past what Pendragon thought might be a kitchen, then up a narrow flight of stairs into a brightly lit hall with garish decoration and crystal globed lamps. A wide double door opened into a large room, furnished in a tawdry fashion, but resembling, in a cheap manner, the ballrooms of the grander upper-class residences. There were three or four men being entertained by tired looking women, obviously hoping for one last customer before exhaustion forced them to seek their sleep. The men barely bothered to glance in the direction

66

of the three newcomers. They passed through the room to a foyer.

"Had a good even' darlings?" asked a rouge-cheeked tart, whose cream dress front was grubby with hand prints. She opened the street door for them. Pendragon could smell musky perfume that failed to disguise sweat as he passed. "Come again, gentlemen. Try a different lady next time. We cater for every taste, remember."

The air was clean now that they were in the streets again and Pendragon took several deep and thankful breaths. He was surprised to recognise the road as Oxford Street.

There was a line of waiting growlers and carriages parked along the kerb, their tired drivers standing together in a close group, chatting quietly. Cragg ignored them and crossed the street to where a tall and narrow coach, of an old-fashioned style, stood in the shadow of a building. The coachman seemed asleep, resting slumped forward on his seat above the coach body. The man jerked himself upright as they arrived, but said nothing.

"Inside, if you please, gentlemen," Cragg ordered, pulling open the coach door. As he climbed in behind the two men the coachman's whip cracked and the vehicle moved. Cragg swore and snapped the coach door closed. It was almost pitch dark inside the vehicle. "Smoked glass," said Cragg. "Useful stuff when you don't want curious eyes looking in, or looking out. Might not be a good idea for you gentlemen to know where you're a going as yet."

The coachman had pressed his horses to a fast trot that matched some rhythm of the ancient coach springs, exaggerating their movement and making the ride as uncomfortable as a small boat on a rough sea. Cragg said nothing more, but pulled his coat collar up around his throat and leant his head back against the upholstery.

In the confines of the carriage Cragg's stench was sickening.

Pendragon stared at the dark glazed windows. Beyond them it was possible to see the flame of the occasional street lamp and dark buildings, as though they were viewed through a deep fog. Perhaps, he thought, in daytime one might be able to see the buildings more clearly, recognise a skyline, but at night it was difficult. Even so he kept his eyes surreptitiously on the windows, and hoped Cox was doing likewise.

After a full hour of driving the carriage stopped and the coachman rapped his whipstock on the roof as a warning to Cragg. Cragg opened the door and peered out. Satisfied that they had reached the coach's destination he climbed down.

"Come along," he said. "We've a walk ahead of us. Keep close behind me or you'll lose the way. It's a full mile and mostly through woods. Watch your steps, for the ground is rough."

Behind them the coachman whipped his horses again, and without so much as a word turned his coach and drove away.

A narrow gate set in an overgrown blackthorn hedge led the men on to a narrow path. It was still too dark to see much of their surroundings, and for some reason Cragg neglected to light his lamp. He knew his route well, only hesitating when it was necessary for him to lead the way around an obstruction, or climb a stile or fence. There were times when Pendragon could see that they were on a path through the woods; silhouettes of trees, even darker than the sky, loomed above, but on occasions the ground underfoot felt heavy and rutted, as though it had been recently ploughed.

The near darkness of the ride in the coach was now an advantage. Pendragon's eyes adjusted rapidly and he could see Cragg's burly figure on the pathway a few yards in front. But what lay ahead of them all he could not guess; the feel of the pistol in his pocket, and Cox's odd grunts as he stumbled or missed his footing behind, were reassuring. Pendragon slowed his pace a little until Cox was close on his heels.

"Any ideas as to where we may be, Cox?" He whispered the question softly.

"A few. One or two things I noticed. I'm pretty certain we travelled north."

Cragg stopped further conversation, immediately and curtly, hissing for silence, then warning them of the possibility they could be mistaken for poachers unless they were quiet on their journey.

The sky was now beginning to lighten with the first pale greyness of dawn, behind heavy clouds. The woods were thinning once more and the pathway reached a tall brickwork wall. Cragg turned left along it and stopped before a narrow wrought-iron gate. He drew a bunch of keys from a pocket and twisted one in the lock. He drove the gate open with a heave of his shoulders and, when Pendragon and Cox had passed through, locked it again behind them. There was a second gate a yard beyond, this time fastened with a long iron bolt secured with a padlock. The men could have been entering the boundaries of a prison. Cragg removed the padlock and led the men through the gate. He snapped the lock back on to the bolt, then turned and stood motionless, listening intently.

Pendragon could hear only the rustle of leaves moving in the light breeze.

"Now I warn you," said Cragg. "Whatever happens when I whistle, stand quite still, no matter what fear you may feel. Make no move or I can't guarantee you'll live long." Before either of the two men could query his remarks, he put his fingers to his teeth, and shrilled a long low whistle that suddenly rose upwards in pitch to finish only just within the range of human hearing.

A second later some animal, dark and sinister in a feline way, slid from a nearby shadow. It was joined by another beast, and from the opposite side of the three men yet another black animal moved. Yellow eyes caught the thin dawn light, staring unwinking and threatening; lips curled back from white fangs.

Cragg made a strange purring sound in the back of his throat and one of the animals slid forward with more the movement of a reptile than a mammal. Cragg reached down as the animal rubbed against his thigh, and scratched at its pointed ears. Another animal joined the first, fawning for Cragg's caresses and attention.

"It's all right," he said to the two men. "Now they know it's me, you'll be safe, though never attempt to pass them on your own. D'you recognise them?"

Pendragon answered him. "I never thought to see them roaming loose in England; snow leopards, or black panthers."

Cragg chuckled and moved forward. The animals drew back and watched them pass. "There are four of them. The other will be around here somewhere. You're right, black panthers they are, from the jungles of Burma. They recognise only one master, and that's Cragg himself. I keep my pets a little hungry, so don't expect them to bite like dogs; as far as they're concerned, any man other than myself is just a good meal."

Ahead now, at the top of a sweeping drive, stood a turreted house; so ancient that by comparison Pendragon's Hampshire manor was modern. Twisted shutters hid every window and gave the place a deserted and derelict appearance. Part of the stonework, crumbling badly above the eaves, was layered with ancient ivy so heavy it hung from the walls like green winding sheets. Lichen coated the broken roof tiles, and turned the unpainted oak of the woodwork a pallid corpse green.

There were dawn sounds as the men approached the arched porchway; a blackbird high in the branches of a nearby elm trilled and was answered. One of the sleek leopards bounded past, so close to Cox's legs his flinch was instinctive. It leapt the five steps to the doorway and stood looking down at them. Cragg raised his arm in a silent threat and the leopard moved aside.

70

The door was unlocked; Pendragon knew the occupants must feel the panthers provided sufficient security. Cragg motioned the two men inside.

* * *

The entrance hall was lit by a dozen candles, almost dead, their distorted stumps held by lumps of old wax on a slab of cracked marble, placed in the centre of a warped trestle table. The candle flames guttered and smoked in the draught. If the outside of the building had looked derelict, the inside was no better than an ancient tomb. Thick dust and the debris of countless years of neglect covered the floor. Laths and plaster which had broken away from the bowed ceilings lay heaped everywhere. Planks which might at some time have supported a tilted staircase lay across the hall, making it seemingly impossible to venture beyond without causing even more of the supports to fall away. The walls stank of damp and the exposed willow laths were coated with a slimy dark fungoid growth.

Cragg took the men through a rickety doorway into an unlit room which seemed no better than the hallway. An old hanging cupboard, perhaps Elizabethan, stood to the right of the doorway. Cragg pulled open the cupboard's door and stepped inside. Light shone out brightly as he did so. "Perhaps you'll find it a little better beyond here," he told them.

* * *

The room in which Pendragon and Cox found themselves could not have been in greater contrast to the earlier parts of the old house. It was some thirty feet in length, and twenty in width. Like the remainder of the house, its ceilings were beamed, but the oak here was sound; black and oiled. The walls were wood panelled, and hung with tapestries, and the floor consisted of great stone flags, layered in the centre with a deeply piled Persian carpet of unquestionable quality and value. In the corners of the farthest end of the room stood two forged iron suits of jousting armour; steel hands grasping lances that reached almost to the oak beams. The farthest wall was hung with a strange banner, a white Saint Andrew's cross on a scarlet field with, in its centre, a huge mailed hand in a lozenge, grasping the shattered bones of a skeleton. Around the banner was a vast collection of European and Eastern weapons, swords, sabres, scimitars and daggers, arranged in a great fan-like display arcing completely around the banner from floor to ceiling and back. Three crystal chandeliers in a line across the wall lit the room and display.

In the centre of the room was an oak table that could comfortably have held twenty guests. At the far end of the vast expanse of oak, in a chair as impressive as a throne, sat a man, his face shadowed by the lighting behind him.

* * *

The man stood. Without speaking, he closed a vellum-paged book he had been reading and stepped forward until he was some three or four yards from the two men. He was tall, even taller than Pendragon, and broad but not heavy. His face was narrow and his eyes so deeply set into their sockets that with the light of the chandeliers still behind him his face was a hollow skull. He was clean-shaven but his hair was long, reaching below his shoulders. His clothing was well-tailored and fashionable, though Pendragon suspected it of foreign manufacture by the narrow width of the collar and the long buttoned velvet cuffs to the sleeves.

The man examined Pendragon and Cox for long seconds before he spoke. His voice was soft, so syrupy that it invited a shudder. "So, you are the would-be assassins?"

Cragg replied. "Easy to find them, like you said, in the Holy Land. Hardly a man in there who didn't know where they were hiding themselves. I told them, with the reward, they were dead if they stayed longer."

"Thank you, Cragg," said the man. He looked at Pendragon, recognising him as the leader of the two. "Cragg is now leaving us." He smiled, the action making his face even more of a death's head. "Have no thoughts of following him without my permission. There is but one visible door from this room and Cragg will be behind it, as well armed as ever; beyond him are the even more dangerous residents whom I believe you will have already met." He turned his back on the two men and walked to his seat again. He pointed at the chairs beside the table. "Sit down, pray. I have no doubt your walk tired you." The man waited until Pendragon and Cox had joined him. "And now, by what name would you like me to address you?"

"I might choose to give none," replied Pendragon.

The man smiled again. "Indeed, that is your prerogative, but it is inconvenient and ungentlemanly for me to refer to you simply as Mister. Perhaps you would prefer a number? Suggest one!"

"I am Hawkhurst," said Pendragon. "This man is Cox."

"And he is dumb?" asked the man sarcastically.

"He is in my employ," replied Pendragon. "And now, Sir, who are you?"

The man clasped his fingers together and pressed his hands down between his knees as though he were stretching in boredom. It was an arrogant gesture that made Pendragon's neck chill with anger.

"Before I answer your question, Hawkhurst," the man said, "let me tell you something about yourself. Firstly, I know by your manner, though certainly not by either your appearance or dress, that you are an educated man of some class. You may disguise all else, but there are certain things which remain obvious. Your voice is of a man used to command, and therefore I suspect a military background, amongst the aristocracy. Your

73

name is not familiar to me other than that of a rather obscure Sussex village, thus I doubt if it is genuine. As for your man Cox, I have no doubt he is what you say; in your employ. I know more, Hawkhurst; that yesterday you attacked Prince Albert's carriage, in Piccadilly, and that you fired your pistol *inside* the carriage. You will notice, Hawkhurst, I do not use the words, attempted to kill. I am, at this moment, of the opinion you did *not* attempt to kill Prince Albert.

"You may have heard of a camera-obscura," he continued. "There was a famous one in the Crystal Palace at the Great Exhibition a few years ago. With it, a viewer could see the panorama of almost all of Hyde Park. Well, Hawkhurst, I have one installed here. I watched you enter by the main gate, and followed your progress up to my door. I have said you have the voice of a man used to command, and you have also the walk, and mannerisms. I have absolutely no doubt of some sort of military career both for yourself and your man. I ask myself this question; if a military man with an obvious army background manages to force his way into an intended victim's coach, how is it that he can miss, with three consecutive bullets, at a range of certainly no more than four feet? When you have answered that question to my satisfaction, Hawkhurst, then perhaps I will give you my name."

Pendragon's mind raced. The man was astute, perhaps too clever. He kept his voice calm. "You're correct about the military background; I have no reason to deny it. I served with the private army of Narsu Pant in Baroda. I was . . ." he paused as though embarrassed. "I was retired when the Bombay Government made certain charges of corruption against me, and returned to England. Cox, I know, was a Sergeant; he deserted a few months ago when his regiment was posted overseas."

"That, I have no doubt, is at least part of the truth." The man looked hard at Pendragon. "Any past experience you may claim of India is easy to check. I spent a little time out there, myself."

Pendragon felt happier. His birth and childhood in Rhotuck, with his father's regiment the 5th Bengal European Cavalry, gave him a far deeper knowledge of the country than any casual visitor might possess. "Should you need to know, Sir, why I missed my shots at Prince Albert, then that too is regrettably simple. This is my pistol." He brought the weapon from his pocket and laid it on the table in front of the man. "You will see it is of foreign manufacture, rather small and by English standards too ornate. It is also of a very modern and untried type; a revolver of five shots, with the cylinder loading from the front. If you have knowledge of this type of weapon you will know the method of loading is as follows: a measured amount of powder is poured in from a flask. On top of this is placed a bullet which is forced down on to the powder by a pivoting arm. Once all the chambers are loaded, it is necessary to coat the entire front of the cylinder with wax to prevent the explosion flashing from one chamber to another as soon as the first shot is fired. Yesterday morning it was raining, and colder than usual. I took care loading the pistol, and then pressed it into my waistband. It remained there for some time. During this period, some of the wax coating, no doubt affected by the weather, was removed by friction against my trouser waistband. When I forced my way into Prince Albert's coach, and pressed the trigger for the first time, three cylinders fired at once. My hand and wrist were bruised and I had the good fortune not to lose a finger. However, the shock threw my aim upwards, and numbed my complete arm. I tried a second and third shot once I got the cylinder past the fired chambers, but by then I was being dragged from the coach by the crowd. Had it not been for Cox here, I would have been apprehended."

The man rubbed a thin finger up the side of a hollow cheek. He picked up the pistol and examined it. "It shows no sign of accident."

"It is cleaned and loaded, as you would expect from an army

75

man." Pendragon pushed his slight advantage. "And now, Sir, if you are satisfied, I would welcome your name."

The man slid the pistol across the table to Pendragon before he spoke. "You will know it already, Hawkhurst," he said. "I am Sir James Helm."

"Helm," repeated Pendragon. Of course, this must be the man Horlm mentioned in Herr Stieber's police report; the ghost had materialised! The discovery gave Pendragon a feeling of satisfaction. However, the name Helm was itself familiar. He probed his memory and was unable to conceal his surprise. "Helm? I remember; James Helm, of Manninghouse. I remember also there was a national scandal. But surely the Earl committed suicide? It was reported an inquest found him dead by his own hand!"

The man opposite chuckled with satisfaction. "Not dead, Hawkhurst; not dead, but simply gone before."

4

HENRY COX HAD BEEN SILENT during Pendragon's conversation with Helm. Now he spoke, with disgust in his voice. "You beat a servant girl to death."

Helm smiled. "Quite right, deserter Sergeant Cox; I beat the girl to death. The evidence subsequently given without any defence did convict me. When a girl is manacled to a barn door, stripped naked, and then beaten to pulp with chains, it is hardly likely even the most senile of courts will give a verdict of accidental death."

"The seventh Earl of Manninghouse was found also dead," added Pendragon, remembering the case vividly described in the columns of *The Times*. "He blew his head off and was found by his butler."

Helm laughed. "Headless bodies are inconsiderately hard to identify, Hawkhurst. How did I arrange it? Quite simply! The man was an out-of-work clerk. I invited him home, gave him a good bath and a suit of my clothes; he was, in fact, grateful at the time. Then I blew off his head while he rested in my bedroom. It was a kindness to the man. It was convenient for me; I had debts which would have taken me two lifetimes to settle. It was a relief to leave them."

"Why are you interested in us?" It took Pendragon an effort to keep the tone of revulsion from his question.

Helm leant forward and stared at Pendragon, coldly. "An intriguing question. I invited you here because I am a specialist in death."

"As your man also claims," said Pendragon.

"Cragg? Yes, I suppose so! He too is interested in death. In fact, Mister Hawkhurst, we are a small group of four men, each of us with the one common factor—we are all interested in death." Helm's voice brightened with a sickening enthusiasm. "Death, Hawkhurst, has become my hobby. Since my, well, exile if you like, I have found death both pleasurable and profitable. Hence the comfort in which I and my colleagues live. We sell death, Mister Hawkhurst. That we enjoy our work is immaterial; our chief concern is reward."

"You still have not explained your interest in my man and myself."

"I have one or two reasons. For a start, may I say my little company needs to be expanded." Helm spoke with satisfaction. "Business continually increases. I keep an eye open for likely employees." He leant towards Pendragon. "Don't imagine, Hawkhurst, that it is easy to find good murderers. London is doubtless full of bad ones, but they are brawlers and cut-throats fit only for the Newgate gallows. Efficient, presentable and educated murderers are hard to come by. My business may be unusual, but like any other it relies for its success not only on demand, but on the high quality of the men I employ. Yes, Hawkhurst, one reason you interest me is as an employee. You may consider, if you like, that you are attending an interview for a post." Helm leant back in his chair and folded his arms across his chest.

"And if the position is offered, what if I should refuse?" Pendragon asked.

Helm laughed again. "My dear Hawkhurst, there is absolutely no question of that happening. If I choose to offer the post, then you will accept; the alternative must be quite clear to you.

I will pass you to Cragg and he will actually thank me, for I can assure you that you are tastier and cheaper than horsemeat. Please, dear fellow, do not even consider a refusal; hope rather that I choose to make the offer."

"And what are your present thoughts on the matter?"

"You may be in luck," said Helm. "You have a certain coolness I find amusing. You have education in your favour, and manners which will be acceptable in any society in which your work may place you. We are an international business and our clients are wealthy and normally influential men. You have courage, as I have heard from the reports of your attack on our German Prince. As for your man, I am, as yet, quite uncertain."

"We work together," Pendragon insisted firmly. "I trust Cox implicitly. He is an expert at arms, and useful."

Helm's eyes hardened suddenly. His face, already pallid, whitened. "Don't try to inflict conditions on me, Hawkhurst. If I say a man dies, then he will die. You may both yet die. It would even give me a certain pleasure to watch you die. Remember, always remember, I *enjoy* death, Hawkhurst." He stiffened as though correcting himself for his loss of control. He was silent for a moment, and then spoke more calmly. "However, you might well need a servant, *if* you are employed. If this man is indeed useful and able to earn his keep, then it is possible he may remain with you." There was a heavy knocking at the door at the far end of the chamber, and Helm relaxed in the great chair and stared down the table. "Yes?"

The door was pushed open and a man entered the room, pausing just inside the door until Helm invited him forward and introduced him.

"This is a colleague, Hawkhurst. One more of us. He calls himself Gaunt; more from a sense of drama, I feel, than truth. Gaunt, this is a possible recruit, a gentleman by the name of Hawkhurst. Hawkhurst is the very one who bungled the attempt on Prince Albert's life, Gaunt." Gaunt nodded at Pendragon.

79

"Gaunt has a number of very useful talents. You will notice a certain air of the nondescript about him. Look at him carefully, Hawkhurst." Helm paused, then continued. "Now turn about, Gaunt." Gaunt did so, turning his back on the seated group. "Now describe him, Hawkhurst."

Pendragon thought of the man's appearance. Helm had been right; apart from Gaunt's height, which was little more than five feet six inches, and his slim build, Pendragon could remember nothing of his features. Even his hair colouring was a common brown. "I believe he is, as you say, unusually nondescript," he admitted at last.

"Quite correct, Hawkhurst," Helm smiled. "Put Gaunt with three or four other men, and he is at once lost from sight. He can disappear at will in the smallest crowd; he is, virtually, an invisible man. You may turn back again, Gaunt, and re-appear for us." Gaunt did so. His face was a complete and expressionless blank, giving no hint as to his inner feelings. "Gaunt has other qualities," said Helm. "He has an outstanding memory. He can visit a building but once, and then, a month later, sketch it with an accuracy which includes every window, every door, passage, and alcove. He can remember the size, shape and design of a key so well that he can file an exact duplicate. He is as silent as Cragg's panthers, and many more times as deadly. He does not kill for money, Hawkhurst. Gaunt kills only for pleasure; his satisfaction is in the writhing, agonised but silent death of his victim, and his own exact skill."

"I have completed my work," said Gaunt in a voice as nondescript as his appearance.

"Good," replied Helm. "Go then, and send in Cragg to take these men to their room." Gaunt left them. Helm watched his going, almost as though he didn't even trust his own safety in the man's presence, before he turned again to face Pendragon. "You will now leave me, Hawkhurst. You will find your room comfortable enough. I regret for the time being it must be locked, but Cragg's own quarters are near by and he will arrange food for you. If you need anything more, then shout for him. You and your man will remain in your room until I send for you with my final decision; it may be several hours yet."

* * *

Pendragon and Cox were alone. The room in which they had been placed seemed to be part of the wing above the hall where they had met Helm. They had reached it by way of a staircase hidden by a sliding section of panel within the hall itself, and Pendragon suspected the entire occupied part of the house was both above and perhaps below the hall. It puzzled him slightly; from his brief look at the outside of the house, there had been no sign of the occupied wing. No doubt a careful and cunning arrangement of the rooms had created an illusion that was a clever disguise. To any viewer, even with a telescope, the hall would appear derelict. Even to one who dared and survived the panthers, the impression actually within the house itself was still one of abandoned disrepair. Only the most minute examination would reveal the real living quarters.

"Well, what do you think?" asked Cox, softly.

"That we should watch our tongues," cautioned Pendragon. "These walls may conceal ears, and even eyes. This is not the time for discussion; we can only wait and learn what is to follow. I believe for certain we will need our strength and having lost a night's sleep we should take this opportunity to rest."

* * *

It was mid-afternoon when Cragg returned to their room and invited Pendragon and Cox to follow him down to the hall, where Helm was waiting with his decision. There seemed to be something amusing Cragg, some idea or thought which he would have liked to tell to them, but was unable or unwilling.

Helm was sitting in his chair at the end of the table, and might well not have moved since they last saw him. As they entered, he ignored them for a few moments, then frowned.

"Have a seat, Captain Pendragon," he said, his eyes cold slits as he lifted his head.

Pendragon smiled grimly. "You were fast to learn my true name."

"Gaunt was quick," corrected Helm. "I warned you of his advantages. Before you met him he spent twenty minutes making a crayon sketch of you through a spy hole. He is an able artist. Had you been a common man, no doubt it might have been impossible for us to find your true identity. But, Captain Pendragon, how many military men who are obviously officers are there in London? Not an impossible number! It was a probability at one time you belonged to a military club, and there are less than a dozen of them. Information regarding you came from the third club Gaunt visited; a steward at the Guards and Cavalry recognised your portrait immediately. For the price of a guinea he told Gaunt much about you. I learn you are Captain John Pendragon; contrary to your story, you were not in the employ of His Highness Narsu Pant, although I believe you were born in India. You were, Captain Pendragon, an officer of the 11th Hussars; Prince Albert's Own! You were heroic at Balaclava and discharged the service as a result of your wounds, and not, as you implied, because of dishonourable conduct. Which brings me to a most important question, and one which I deliberately saved until I learned your true identity. What, Captain Pendragon, was the reason for your attempt on the life of Prince Albert? Why should you desire to take the life of the man who is your regiment's Colonel in Chief? Think well before you answer; it is the difference between your life and your death!"

Pendragon answered coolly and with as little hesitation as possible. He made his voice soft and casual. "I, too, like yourself, offer my services for reward," he said. "On this occasion, Helm, I am employed by a German gentleman, Count Erik Von Oberstein."

* * *

For the second time since their initial meeting, Helm showed visible and uncontrolled emotion. His face tautened; his lips drew back into an almost feline snarl. He clenched his fists until his knuckles whitened. There was no doubt the man was as dangerous as the leopards he kept to guard himself.

Cragg, who had been standing a little distance from the table, swore under his breath and began a question. "But what . . ."

"Silence," spat Helm. He stared at Pendragon. "So your employer is Count Von Oberstein, Captain Pendragon. Your statement surprises me. I do not intend, at this moment, to call you a liar or to enlighten you further. It is sufficient if I say it appears our interests clash. The matter will, however, be resolved shortly. You will remember I told you my company consists of four? Three of them you have met. The other man is presently abroad, but is expected in London this evening. Cragg will be meeting him at the Dover railway terminus in the Bricklayer's Arms Station at eight o'clock. With my man, providing everything is progressing as arranged, will be Count Von Oberstein, Captain Pendragon! Should he verify your story, then I will insist you join us. Should he deny your claimed connection, then I guarantee your death personally at my hands. And I tell you, Captain Pendragon, it will be a death so slow and terrible that even you are incapable of imagining its form." Helm paused. He was sweating and his forehead glistened in the glow of the candles, which even in daytime were the room's only source of light. "Cragg, take these two gentlemen back to their quarters. Make certain they are quite secure. This evening will undoubtedly prove to be interesting. But first, Cragg, search ex-Sergeant Cox for weapons; Captain Pendragon, your pistol, Sir."

* * *

Once Cragg had left Pendragon and Cox in their room, and had slid the bolt across the door on the outside, Pendragon rubbed his hands together in satisfaction. He waited until Cragg's footsteps disappeared down the staircase and then spoke softly. "It couldn't have been better, Cox. By nine o'clock this evening, all the birds will be here in the coop—with an extra bonus, Von Oberstein himself. Undoubtedly our German cousins will be pleased to see him back in the fatherland, after his arrest."

Cox nodded. He was finding little comfort in Pendragon's satisfaction. "Only one thing, though, Captain. We're in the pen as well! I don't think it's going to be very healthy here once that German arrives."

"How long would you say it would take a man with a carriage to reach the Kent Road from here?" asked Pendragon.

"A good hour."

"Then if Cragg is to meet his friends at eight o'clock, he will leave here by a quarter to seven at the latest."

"I would think so, Sir."

"Good. We shall leave here at seven," said Pendragon.

"Leave? Blimey, Captain, leave, just like that? You make it sound easy to walk through a garden full of hungry leopards. I've seen one of those things tear a tentful of men into shreds, on the frontier; there's more than one in the garden, and we don't have any weapons."

"Weapons, no," agreed Pendragon, "but I believe we might just have the best protection possible. It will be a case of keeping our nerves steady, and our true feelings hidden. In the meantime, we will spend the time in loosening and removing the door hinges, in preparation for our departure. You will find my

84

pocket knife behind you, hidden under the cushion of that chair. You have it? Good! A most un-British weapon, Cox, but a useful tool at times."

* * *

If it had been an uncomfortable and dangerous twenty-four hours for Pedragon and Cox, it was as embarrassing for Page Cloverly. At the moment he gave little for his chances of remaining employed in his post in the Home Office.

Pendragon's attack on the Prince's coach had produced, from Cloverly's point of view, unpleasant and difficult results. Once the Prince himself had been found to be safe and unharmed, the personal guards of the Household Cavalry had re-formed under the direction of their officer. It was the officer's intention to return at once to Buckingham Palace, where he felt sure the Prince would need some slight rest to recover from the apparently narrow escape. The Prince, however, decided otherwise. It was his duty, he told the young officer, to continue as though nothing had happened. He was unhurt, unscathed, he said, and considerably unimpressed by the amateurish attack by the would-be assassin. The young officer, overwhelmed by the Royal courage, dared not disagree. It was unfortunate he had already despatched a rider to the palace, with a report of the incident!

Within minutes of the messenger's arrival at Buckingham Palace, the Queen's carriage had been made ready and a full company of battle-armed Household Cavalry sat waiting, in their saddles, in the front courtyard. The coach swept by them at a canter, forcing their officers to shout hurried orders. The troopers galloped their mounts in some confusion, to place themselves around their monarch's coach before it left the palace gates. There was considerable disarray for several hundred yards of the route up the Mall before order was eventually established.

To the populace who used Saint James's park for their midday promenades, and the street traders and pedestrians nearer Trafalgar Square, it appeared that a stampede of cavalry mounts was thundering its way towards them. The crowds stopped, open mouthed, and watched as a hundred and twenty cavalrymen surrounding a Royal coach hammered into the square, the coach's wheels showering sparks from the granite surfaces of the cobbles. Instead of the parade moving at an accustomed pace while traffic ahead of it was cleared, this time it wove its way between carriages and traders' carts, the cavalrymen shouting wildly, and the normal road-users swerving their vehicles in terror from the paths of the troops.

There was a melee of cavalry horses and dismounting officers in front of the National Gallery. The coach slid to a halt amongst them. A diminutive and pregnant figure leapt from the carriage, ignoring the arm of the attendant officer. She trotted up the steep steps surrounded by sabre-carrying cavalrymen who made hard work of following her with their stiff leather thigh boots and steel armour breastplates. Spurs rang against the stonework, harness and decorative chain jingled. Startled gallery officials were swept aside by high-pitched Royal command.

What transpired in the conversation between husband and panic-stricken wife, behind the gallery doors, is not recorded. What was certain, however, was that during the tears and the scolding, Prince Albert disclosed, for the first time, the full details of the plan to which he was accomplice.

* * *

At just after noon on the next day Page Cloverly received an ominous summons to attend Buckingham Palace immediately, and to report at once to the offices of Field Marshal Sir Hubert Gowers, the Queen's equerry. For several minutes after his announcement and entry to the equerry's office, the Field Marshal said nothing. His silence was ferocious; he paced angrily back and forth in front of Page Cloverly. When eventually he spoke, he hissed the word like an angry viper. "You blithering idiot, Cloverly. I never believed I'd see the day when I thought such words would be mine to describe the actions of the Head of Her Majesty's Internal Security Force. What madness made you agree to such a thing? And how could you actually persuade the Prince himself the action was necessary? Madness and foolishness, every piece of it! Her Majesty is raging furious; I've never seen her so angry. She will not even so much as look at Prince Albert, let alone pass the time of day with him. Great Heavens! When she learnt of the attack, she believed the Prince dead, or at the least seriously wounded. She could have died of the shock. My God, man, don't you know she's pregnant?"

Page Cloverly spent the next twenty minutes explaining the whole purpose of the plot to Sir Hubert Gowers. When he had finished, he added he suppposed he should now tender his resignation.

Sir Hubert Gowers almost exploded. "Resign? Damn me, no Sir! Allow you to resign? I would kill myself first, Sir! Resign you shall not!" He clenched his fists and leant forward until his florid face was within inches of Cloverly. When he spoke, he showered him with fine spittle. "You, Sir, you will justify your foolishness. You had better prove to me, and to Her Majesty, that your action was one based on calculated thought. Pray, Sir, that your plan works, and you safely deliver the would-be assassins for their execution. Should this incredibly stupid idea of yours actually succeed, then I will consider your resignation. But if it fails . . . I warn you, Sir, you will not resign. It is far more likely that you will rot in Newgate if it is within my powers." Sir Hubert Gowers pointed to the door. "Now get out," he shouted.

The afternoon air was ice cold against Page Cloverly's damp forehead as he stepped weakly into the courtyard. He felt like some ten-year-old schoolboy released from a headmaster's interview. Silently he prayed for success, realising with embarrassed guilt the prayer was not to God, but to John Pendragon, wherever he might be.

* * *

It took Pendragon and Cox two hours to free the door hinges from the oak surround. The wood holding the screws might have been ancient, but rather than softening the timber the years had turned it iron hard. Once the hinges were free and it was obvious one or two hard pulls would wrench the door open, Pendragon glanced at his pocket watch.

"Fifteen minutes to six, Cox. If I'm right, then we may expect our friend Cragg to return to his room for his outdoor clothes within the next hour. We must hope he is confident with our security and does not enter here."

Cox looked at the door hinges now hanging loose away from the woodwork. If the door was unlocked from the outside, it would collapse. "And if he does, Captain?"

"Then I fear we are in for a fight. Noise will alert the household, so it must be silent work with fists, and the knife."

It was a further twenty minutes before Pendragon heard movement somewhere below them in the house; footsteps, so heavy that they could only be Cragg's, mounted the old staircase. Pendragon tensed himself as the sounds paused outside the oak door, but a second later they moved on and Cragg's door slammed.

Pendragon counted minutes and tried to imagine Cragg's actions within the room only a few yards away, then the man's door was opened again and the footsteps returned.

Pendragon heard Cragg clear his throat and spit, and then his voice sounded just beyond the oak door. "Captain Pendragon?"

"Yes," answered Pendragon. He looked at Cox who had

moved into position beside the door, and who was now holding the knife ready in his hand.

"Ah," said Cragg, and chuckled. "It'll please you to know I'm away to fetch your employer, Captain. I wish you pleasant future reunions." Cragg laughed without humour, and the two men heard him turn and clump his way down the stairs.

"We'll give him another half an hour," said Pendragon. "I suspect there are two ways in to the grounds; the way we were led, through the woods, and another way by road. It is possible our coach dropped us near the woods as there may have been something we could have recognised nearer the manor; a milestone, a folly, or some sort of landmark. There is no doubt the coach we travelled in was their own, and so there must be a coach-house and stables. I believe they will be near the main gate, wherever that may be. With those leopards roaming loose in the grounds, I doubt if the horses are ever actually brought within the walls. We must give Cragg time to be well on his way. It's near dusk now, and will be dark in a while."

"Leopards can see in the dark," Cox warned apprehensively, "far better than you or I, Captain."

"Perhaps," Pendragon smiled. "I fear I am again gambling with both our lives, Cox. It is my bet that the animals rely more on scent than on appearance. I hope to God I am right."

* * *

"Now," grunted Pendragon. He and Cox jerked hard against the oak door. It dropped slightly and pivoted inwards; the lock on its right side screeched as rivets tore from the metal. Pendragon paused, but there was no sound beyond in the crumbling house. A few yards away was Cragg's room. Pendragon hoped the man's door was unlocked, and was relieved when it swung open silently as he raised the latch. The room was in a filthy condition and it was obvious Cragg either considered it only temporary accommodation, or was quite used to living in the squalid mess. The room stank of unwashed clothing. Cragg's bed, in the far corner of the room, was nothing more than a heap of reeking sacking on a straw-stuffed mattress.

Cox's nose wrinkled. "God, Captain! It smells like the animal cages at the zoological gardens. Worse, perhaps."

"His uncleanliness suits our purpose well. Take a look around the room, Cox. Find clothes for both of us; boots as well, if he has some."

"Clothes for us, Captain?" Cox was horrified.

"The thought of using Cragg's clothing is quite as repugnant to me as it is to you," said Pendragon, amused by Cox's reaction. "His filth is to our advantage. I believe, Cox, that the beasts outside will be confused. Though they may not recognise us, I hope the stink of Cragg will prevent them from attacking, at least long enough for us to reach the wall. If we remain here until Von Oberstein arrives, then we are dead men anyway."

Cox stooped and picked up a shirt that was little more than a rag. He held it towards Pendragon with a look of distaste. "I fear, Captain, that if we survive the leopards we may die later of camp fever."

* * *

Cragg's filthy clothing hung from the two men like grotesque carnival attire. The man was so huge it would have been possible for both of them to stand within one of his coats. Cox, who had actually visibly shuddered when Pendragon insisted that even his own underclothing should be removed, grumbled about regimental scrubbings and other dire things he would have arranged for Cragg had the man ever served in his troop.

"Ready?" asked Pendragon.

"Yes, Captain, though I swear I'll soak in a bath for a week once we get home, Sir."

* * *

90

Pendragon had hoped for darkness, but the autumn dusk seemed prolonged. From the crumbling doorway of the house he could see clearly across the overgrown lawns to the thickening trees beyond. It was a wide stretch of open ground, but one they would have to cross whichever way they left the house. There was little enough time left, now; too little to wait until the last light had completely faded.

"Whatever happens, Cox, don't run. Remember, a cat will chase a running mouse. Walk slowly and confidently; don't hesitate or show any fear. We'll stay close to each other." Pendragon paused for a second, then began walking towards the trees. Cox hesitated, squared his shoulders, tucked in his chin and followed him.

There were no signs of any of the leopards as the two men walked carefully, slowly and as silently as possible down the steps of the house, and toward the distant trees. For a few moments, Pendragon wondered if, contrary to Cragg's warning, the animals were in fact normally caged.

"Christ!"

Pendragon heard Cox's near silent exclamation. From the shadows beneath the trees, still sixty yards ahead of them, bounded a black shape. Pendragon braced himself as the leopard increased its speed until it seemed to be covering the ground at an impossible rate. He could see its eyes now, terrifying and evil yellow slits; its mouth was a snarl exposing glistening white teeth that Pendragon had no difficulty imagining tearing into his flesh. At the last second of its charge, when it was within feet of the two men, the leopard swerved, its claws raking long black grooves in the grass. Pendragon took a deep breath and kept walking. The leopard circled the men, its ears flattened against its gleaming black skull, its muscles rippling beneath the sleek fur.

The trees were nearer now; a few more yards and the two men would at least be safe from observation from the house. Just as

91

they reached the first of the dark shadows, a nerve-ripping snarl sounded from the branches above them, and a second leopard dropped silently to the ground a yard from them. It squatted back on its haunches and snarled again. Pendragon felt the hair of his neck bristle, and forced himself to ignore the animal, walking past within inches of its muzzle. The first of the animals was now close against Cox's side, and Pendragon could see Cox's face pale, even in the poor light.

There was a sharp-edged, dark silhouette ahead of the men. The wall, thought Pendragon, thankfully. Once it was reached then they must follow it until at some point they found the double gate through which they had first entered the grounds.

Beneath the trees it was now almost full darkness and the two leopards were moving like black silk, near the men's legs. There was a scuffling sound ahead of them. Pendragon's palms were moist as he clenched them.

Helm's voice was arrogant, confident and amused. "Captain Pendragon, and his man Sergeant Cox, out for a stroll? Good evening, gentlemen. Stop, and remain perfectly still. I see you are accompanied by two of the animals; there are a further two, here at my feet ahead of you. I also have an eight-bore shotgun, loaded with deer ball, aimed at the Captain's chest. At this range, even in poor light, I fear I cannot miss." The man's voice was slightly muffled.

"Helm," said Pendragon, angrily. Damn the man and his luck, he thought.

"You're a fortunate man, Captain. No one has ever succeeded in leading these animals so far; few survive the first ten yards from the building. I do believe you have bewitched them in some remarkable manner. But for my watchfulness you might have shown me a clean pair of heels." The voice hardened slightly. "Carelessness, Captain Pendragon. You forgot my camera obscura. How stupid of you. Such an eminent military gentleman, too."

"I made the mistake of thinking it a toy with which you played only occasionally," admitted Pendragon, now furious at his oversight.

"Toy?" Helm laughed. "A toy would hardly be fitted with such fine and costly lenses, Captain. From its vantage point on the highest part of the roof, the image is reflected down and then projected on to a screen hidden behind a panel in my hall. By rotating the camera by means of a machine, I can examine any part of my grounds, and do so frequently when I have guests. I was expecting you to make some sort of a move, Captain, for I place little faith in the story you are employed by Count Von Oberstein. It was simply a matter of me waiting until you tried to escape. You might call it an amusement. I wondered if the leopards would kill you, or if you would outwit them. You had *no* chance of outwitting me!"

"What now, Helm?" asked Pendragon.

"A slight problem, Captain Pendragon. I have a house guest I am sure you will wish to meet. This, of course, necessitates your return. The difficulty, Captain, is simply I am quite uncertain as to whether I can prevent Cragg's leopards from killing you on our route back. You see, Captain, I am protected from them; I *do not* control them. And I can assure you I would not kill them to save either of you. Perhaps you should throw your Sergeant Cox to them, then run while they savage him." Helm laughed, and moved slightly forward until Pendragon could see him.

As the man had said, the remaining two leopards were beside him, and moved as he moved. Helm's entire body and head glistened strangely in the poor light. He seemed to read Pendragon's mind. "My protection, Captain. One might call it a form of armour, though it is too light to stop even an arrow, let alone a bullet. There are times when I wish to move about my grounds, and leopards are such singular animals even I found

93

them beyond me. It is the one gift that Cragg possesses; compensation for his lacking in all else, no doubt. This suit of mine, Captain, is of light plates of bright iron. Each plate, as you may observe, is set with a two-inch spike which the leopards find unpleasant in their jaws. I was attacked the first time I ventured from the house, but the beasts learnt their lesson admirably. I pass through them, Captain, because I have proved myself inedible. Now turn around, and begin your walk back. I suggest, if you believe in any form of God, that you begin praying for assistance."

The walk back to the house seemed even longer than when the two men had left. The four leopards moved beside them, crossing and recrossing their paths, sometimes seeming calm, whilst at other moments they bristled with anger as though about to attack. At the times when they seemed fiercest and angriest, Helm would chuckle with satisfaction as though he hoped the animals would attack the two men. There was no doubt it was the strong smell of Cragg on the men's clothing that protected them and Pendragon was glad, for once, of the man's uncleanliness. There was no doubt the animals became angry and confused as the unfamiliar scent of Pendragon and Cox reached them.

Once they had entered the hall of the building, and Helm had closed the huge door behind them, Pendragon heard Cox make a sigh of relief.

"Excellent," said Helm. "I recognise your bravery, gentlemen. Now go through to my hall." He followed them. "Ah, of course, Captain Pendragon, I see now how you managed to deceive the beasts. Very clever of you. I thought you smelt unpleasantly familiar; Cragg is not the most hygienic of men. He was careless to allow this to happen, and I shall reprimand him later." Helm, still keeping his shotgun aimed at Pendragon, pulled the spike studded casque from his head and tossed it on to a chair, then he slipped out of the armoured top-coat and unfastened his iron leggings. "Quite uncomfortable, Captain Pendragon," he explained, "though effective." He straightened his clothing, laid the shotgun on the table within easy reach of his hands, and sat himself in his customary seat. "You may sit down, Captain Pendragon." He nodded towards the chair at the far end of the long table. "Far enough away, if you please, to enable me to breathe clean air. I would like now to introduce you to my house guest." Helm reached sideways and jerked at a bell cord. He leant back in his chair and folded his arms.

Von Oberstein, thought Pendragon. He wondered briefly what the man would be like; not that it mattered. Helm seemed quite certain Pendragon could not be employed by the German. Perhaps, thought Pendragon, the German Count had arrived earlier than expected and Cragg's journey had been no more important than part of the titillation of Helm's warped sense of humour.

Helm picked up the shotgun again, and aimed its barrels steadily at Pendragon's chest. For a fraction of a second Pendragon wondered if Helm was about to kill him. He heard the door behind him open.

Helm moved the muzzle of the gun. "You may turn around and look, Captain Pendragon."

Pendragon turned. What he saw so startled him that despite Helm's shotgun he leapt to his feet, his chair crashing to the floor.

"My God! Georgina!"

5

HELM'S MIRTHLESS AND CRUEL LAUGH echoed in the long hall. Pendragon was beside Georgina in three long strides. He took her by the shoulders. She seemed dazed, her green eyes strangely flat. As he touched her she jerked back instinctively, then recovered herself.

"Have they harmed you?" asked Pendragon, urgently.

She shook her head, then looked at his filthy clothing. "I didn't recognise you." Her voice was childlike and apologetic. "They . . . brought me here a while ago. Why, John? What's happening?"

Pendragon swung round to face Helm, his fists clenched in anger, but Helm, still laughing, brought up the shotgun again and Pendragon found himself staring down its ominous barrel.

"Your beautiful aunt, the Miss Carr," said Helm. "You see, Captain Pendragon, we found out quite a lot about you; even the object you apparently hold most precious." His voice sharpened. "We are not amateurs, Captain Pendragon, nor are we primitives lacking in both education and intelligence to be swamped by your mere waving of a spurious banner. You have chosen a dangerous game, and I doubt you are yet familiar with its rules."

"You bastard!'" swore Pendragon.

Helm ignored the insult. "Gaunt, bring the lady to the table and have her seated. You too, Captain Pendragon. Sit at the head, where I can watch you. Gaunt, stay and guard the Captain's man; by the colour of his face he may feel inclined to act foolishly." There was a sound beyond the door and Helm looked up and nodded a greeting. "Von Oberstein. You choose an opportune moment to grace us with your presence. Please remove your cloak and join us; you too, Selwyn."

Cragg and two men had entered the room. Cragg himself stepped back until he was nothing more than a bulky shadow behind Cox. The taller of the two men, his hair cropped closer than an Englishman's, moved to the table, swinging his cloak from his shoulders and dropping it casually across the back of one of the chairs. The second man, slim and neatly dressed, waited until the German Count had seated himself before he spoke.

"Cragg explained about this man on the way here. I believe he has claimed to be in the employ of Count Von Oberstein. The Count will deny the fact. We need waste no more time with him. Give him to Cragg for his pets."

The German spoke, looking at Pendragon with curiosity. His accent was thick and difficult to understand although he used his grammar with skill. "Wait. No need to kill him yet. There are questions I want answered, important questions. He seems to know far too much, this English Captain."

"I agree absolutely, Gentlemen," smiled Helm. "He knows far too much. But, Count Von Oberstein, I will be grateful if you will permit me to deal with the present situation. I have had a few hours to consider the matter carefully." He turned to Pendragon. "If you so much as move a muscle, Captain Pendragon, then Gaunt, who is standing behind you, will draw his razor across your throat. You will be dying before you get to your feet. I have no idea whether you have ever watched a stuck pig die, but I can assure you its bloody struggles are not graceful."

97

Pendragon felt the steel of a blade pressed against the side of his throat. Helm continued. "Cragg, deal with the Captain's man." There was a movement Pendragon could see from the corner of his eye, and the sound of a sharp blow. Georgina gasped as Cox slumped to the floor. "Good," said Helm. "Now, Captain Pendragon, you are going to explain exactly who you are, and what you are trying to do." He paused for a few seconds as Pendragon remained silent, then spoke to Cragg again. "Cragg, take hold of Miss Carr and strip her naked. Don't move, Captain, or you are dead, and once we have killed you, there is no reason for us to keep the attractive Miss Carr alive."

Pendragon spoke between his clenched teeth. "I'll tell you what you want to know if you guarantee no harm will come to her."

Helm laughed. "There you are, Count Von Oberstein, a typical example of the English gentleman." Helm sounded pleased. "Had we tortured him, he would not even have gasped as we tore out his bowels. But threaten to dishonour his loved ones and you have an immediate reaction. British officers are usually quite predictable in attitudes toward their females; had we offered to carve the liver from his man Cox, no doubt he would have silently allowed us to do so."

Count Von Oberstein's eyes narrowed. He stared coldly at Pendragon. "You will answer my questions, Captain. You will answer them correctly and in every detail. I wish to know in what official capacity you are operating. Official it must be, for there is no private reason for your actions, nor any accidental way in which you could have learnt my name in connection with this matter."

"Say nothing, John; say nothing at all. I . . ." Georgina's voice was again normal and showed no fear.

"Be silent, Miss Carr, or I will order Cragg to remove your tongue. Now speak quickly, Captain Pendragon," warned Helm. "I see from an animal look in Cragg's eyes, and the way in which

98

he moistens his lips, that he is anticipating great enjoyment from his games with Miss Carr's slim body."

Pendragon glanced at Georgina apologetically. "I am a Queen's Agent," he said softly.

Cragg swore in the background.

"As I suspected," breathed Von Oberstein with satisfaction. "Now you may kill him, Herr Helm."

"Wait." Helm stopped Cragg's movement. "First, what proof, Captain? It is known all Queen's Agents carry secret identity. Move very slowly, and produce it."

Pendragon put his hand inside his waistband and felt for his narrow money belt. He drew out the thin platinum identity warrant and slid it along the table. Helm trapped the glistening metal plate with the flat of his hand, picked it up and held it to the light. "Well. So this is a Queen's Agent's warrant." He read the engraved lettering and examined the Royal cipher carefully. "Impressive, Captain Pendragon. Had I known I harboured such an important guest, I would have arranged better accommodation. Now tell us more, Captain . . . no, do not tell us more, simply tell me if I am wrong. The assassination attempt was a move to put you in contact with us, correct? Which means the British government is fully aware that someone intends to kill Prince Albert. This means that you outwitted us in the first round, which annoys me, Captain." Helm paused again. "However the remaining rounds are certainly ours, for Cragg assures me that you were not followed from the rookery. Furthermore, you have no idea where you are at this time. There is no way in which you can have contacted any of your friends, so they have no idea of our identity, although they obviously have knowledge of Count Von Oberstein's part in this business."

"In the name of God," swore Von Oberstein, "kill them. We waste time and they are a danger to us alive. Get rid of them now and new plans can be made. There are other methods by which we can reach our aims. The death of Albert Saxe Coburg is important, but not absolutely imperative."

Helm turned quickly on the German. "Not imperative perhaps to you, dear Count, but important enough to me. You have contracted a business with us, and I intend to see it completed. There shall be no withdrawals by either side."

"The risk is now too great," insisted Von Oberstein. "I am a politician; if the assassination of Prince Albert risks the safety of the remainder of my organisation then I cannot permit it to take place."

Helm smiled coldly. "There is no risk, Von Oberstein. We now have a situation we could never manufacture for ourselves. Were I to ask Captain Pendragon to murder his Queen he would refuse, even though we killed all his family before his eyes. I believe, however, that the German Prince is another kettle of fine fish. The Prince is a man, and furthermore, he is not the British sovereign, nor will he ever be. Pendragon is quite aware we will kill the man, if not now, then at some future date. And so, Count Von Oberstein, Captain Pendragon will himself assassinate the Prince. What better man to do so? He has access to the Prince himself. No one will suspect him. He will kill Prince Albert, will you not, Captain Pendragon?"

"He will never agree," said Von Oberstein. "He will think of his honour."

Pendragon remained silent.

Helm folded his arms across his chest and stared down the table at him. "It is his honour upon which I count. Captain Pendragon, think well of your honour at this moment. Let me refresh your memory of a few games that can be played with the female body. There is one which, I believe, originated in Spain during the inquisition; they call it the Rape of Saint Jaquila. One of the victim's feet is anchored to the floor, while the other is tied to a rope passing through a pulley on the ceiling. The rope through the pulley is weighted until the naked victim attains a position which would be of credit even to the finest of our prima ballerinas. Whilst so fastened, interesting things may be done to her person which, I am informed, include an assault with heated . . ."

"Enough, Helm," shouted Pendragon. "We have no need of your disgusting repertoire of torture."

"Believe me, there is much more," promised Helm. He pressed the tips of his fingers together. "My goodness, Captain Pendragon, but your aunt looks quite pale. I fear she is about to faint. Perhaps you are right; it may indeed be unnecessary for me to reiterate other ideas which easily come to my mind. I see by your face, Captain Pendragon, that you intend to agree to my suggestion for the present, at least. I am not so foolish as to believe you will not try to plan our downfall—if you can do so without causing your dear aunt suffering. However let me assure you, Captain Pendragon, that suffer she will, at the first move you make which threatens us. She will die in the most prolonged and terrible agony. She will be degraded in every possible way. Your man, pah, he is nothing; but he will die also. In the event of your failure, every member of your household, Miss Carr's household, will be killed. Believe me, Captain Pendragon, when I tell you my threats are as certain as any churchman's holy pledge."

Georgina spoke again. Her voice was pitched fractionally higher, but Pendragon recognised it as a note of anger. "I do not know who you are," she spat the words at Helm, "but I know you are not even fit to be classed a man. You misjudge us badly if you think that your threats may in any way terrify us into assisting you in your foul deeds. If you imagine for one second that any form of torture to my person would influence Captain Pendragon to commit so disgraceful and heinous a crime as an assassination, then . . ."

"Selwyn . . ." Helm's voice interrupted Georgina's harangue. "Bring her to the table. Gaunt, press your razor a little harder against the Captain's jugular vein so he may know the slightest movement will bring about his own death." Helm paused until Georgina was standing beside him, her arms pinioned within Selwyn's hands.

"I warn you, Helm," began Pendragon.

"You warn me not at all, Captain. Dead you are no threat. Selwyn, put one of the lady's hands on the table in front of me."

Georgina struggled, but against Selwyn's masculine strength her movements were futile. He grasped one of her wrists and moved her arm until her hand was palm down on the polished oak surface.

Helm reached to Selwyn's waistband and drew out a bone-handled Spanish knife. He pressed some hidden button and an eight-inch blade shot open. With deliberate slowness he lowered the edge until it was against the joint of Georgina's little finger and hand. He pressed.

Pendragon shouted in rage and horror, and despite the threat of the keen blade against his own throat, sprang forward. Something smashed against the side of his head. His last sight of the scene, as he lost consciousness, was a spurt of deep red blood from Georgina's hand.

* * *

The voice was familiar, and yet strange; distant, as though it called him, in a foreign echo, from some deep abyss. He was dreaming; the tentacles of nightmare clawed him into a horrifying morass. His name: the voice called again, urgently, closer.

"Captain Pendragon, Captain . . ."

The battlefield, the surgeon's tent, the pain! Pendragon sought for reality, fighting his way towards it as a drowning man struggles to bring his head above the dark surface of the sea. Waves scattered to mist.

"Captain Pendragon, Sir . . . look, he's moving! Give him more air."

"He should be indoors, not out here in the stable," said a woman anxiously. "Dear me, look at the poor man."

Pendragon opened his eyes. The scene swayed in front of him. Featureless pink blobs moved on heavy bodies. He forced his eyes to focus; leather harness hung a few inches from his chest, the brasses polished and gleaming in lantern light. The pink blobs became faces, frowning with concern.

"Captain, Sir, it's us. Me, Captain, Ted Blower, Sir." Pendragon struggled to sit up, but the young man held his shoulders. "No, Sir. Best you don't move yourself a while. Kurt's gone for the doctor and he'll be here soon. You're in our stables, Sir. God, we've been a worried for you, Captain."

Pendragon allowed himself to sink back on to the padding of straw. A hand passed him a mug of water, while another lifted his head slightly so he could drink. He recognised one of the housemaids. The water was iced silk. He drank thirstily.

"How long have I been here?" he whispered.

Ted Blower answered. "Not too long, we'd say, Captain. I was here checking the horses but an hour since, and you wasn't here then. The groom heard a moanin' just twenty minutes ago, and then we found you. By the blood on the stones of the yard, it would seem you crawled here."

"What time is it?" asked Pendragon. The scene swirled. He fought to retain consciousness.

Ted Blower held a pocket watch to the lantern. "A little after midnight, Captain."

The unreality of nightmare sucked at Pendragon again. Was it, after all, some terrible dream? Sewers, beggars, leopards and the sound of pistol shots kaleidoscoped within his brain. Darkness took him.

*　*　*

He awoke later as though from a normal but deep sleep. He moved a hand and felt warm linen.

103

There was a voice again, but this time softer, less harsh. "John?"

He opened his eyes and recognised Page Cloverly sitting beside his bed.

"Thank God," breathed Page. "You had us all worried. Can you speak, John?"

Pendragon grimaced. "Better than I can think, at this moment." His throat was dry and as he moved his head pain sparked sharp arrows of light across his eyes. He winced and felt at a bandaged pad across his left ear.

"Whoever struck you, struck fiercely," said Page Cloverly. "The blow bruised your scalp badly and we feared it might have fractured the skull. However the doctor assures us you have no serious injury, perhaps only concussion. You need a good rest, but you'll be as sound as ever in a few days." The tone of his voice became serious. "But before I can let you rest, John, I must know of anything you have learnt, so the department may act.'"

"Act?"

"The assassination attempt; did that mad plan of yours bring any result?"

"Result?" Pendragon paused. "Result?" His memory, his mind, seconds ago calm, whirlpooled in violence. Georgina! That bastard Helm! He tried to swing himself from the bed, but the effort sickened him and made him retch.

Page Cloverly moved to restrain him, horrified. "John? What's the matter?"

"Georgina! The murdering devil's got Georgina."

Page Cloverly held his shoulders. "Nonsense, John, you're confused. Georgina is quite safe; she's not even in London. I have seen a note from her saying she is visiting a relation in Brighton for a few days and will return shortly."

Pendragon shrugged away Cloverly's hands and steadied himself against a bedpost. "You're wrong, Page. I saw her with them. They kidnapped her, and . . . dear God!" The final memory slotted into place; the long blade of Helm's knife pressing down on Georgina's hand. "God!" He forced himself to his feet, his eyes wild. "Page . . . just before one of the swine hit me, I remember they were mutilating her!"

* * *

"Dear Lord, what a terrible mess," breathed Page Cloverly, horrified, when Pendragon had finished his explanations. "Poor Georgina, and I am to blame. I should never have agreed to the plan. On reflection, it was almost certain that if you were discovered recriminations would be effected on the household. That Georgina herself should be involved in such a terrible manner is unthinkable. A search must be carried out at once, even if it means the use of a whole London-based regiment. Prince Albert will agree. There is not another second to waste."

"No." Pendragon spoke firmly. "There must be no large scale attempt at rescue. Such an action will certainly ensure Georgina's immediate death. Helm is a barbarian, Page; he will kill her at the slightest excuse." Pendragon paused. "I was obviously carried here; I couldn't have made the journey on my own, semiconscious. I was almost certainly dumped from a coach at the yard entrance. It is therefore also certain that Helm believes I will now do his bidding rather than risk Georgina's life. To a degree he is right. I am prepared, to an extent, to do his bidding . . ."

Page Cloverly stared at Pendragon, horrified. "And kill the Prince?"

Pendragon shook his head, wryly, ignoring the sharp pains as he did so. "No, not kill the Prince, Page. Helm underestimates my loyalty. Nothing would force me to such dishonour. I will appear to do his bidding; it is essential, in order to keep Georgina alive. He will certainly have one of his spies watching me, watching this house. The spy will report my comings and goings. I suspect, whoever he is, that he will contact me within the next few hours. Well, I'll give the man something to satisfy Helm, at least for a little while. Meantime, Helm has made one mistake which I swear will lead to his downfall. He has removed from my shoulders the cloak of a gentleman. I will hunt him down now, Helm and his company, by whatever method I can use. And if it is in my power to do so, then I will kill them all with as little feeling as I would have in treading upon a bunch of maggots."

6

"Prince Albert must not be informed of all this," insisted Pendragon. "The less interference we have from anyone, the better my chances of carrying the matter through successfully." His head ached abominably and the present conversation was doing nothing to improve it.

Page Cloverly tightened his lips. "I'm sorry, John, but it is already quite out of my hands. I had strict orders yesterday to keep His Highness informed of everything that happened. He was told, early this morning, that you had returned. He knows also the extent of your injuries, but insists on an immediate report in person. We have a summons to attend the palace as soon as you are able to dress and travel. We are to go directly to Gowers's offices."

"Damn and blast!" swore Pendragon. "Gowers! He's about the last man in the world who should know of our dealings. He was a fool in the Napoleonic War, and an even greater and older one in the Crimea. The man's in his dotage! I can tell you his reaction now; leave the woman where she is, and send in the troops. Surround the place, wherever it may be, with field artillery, and blast it from the ground." He banged his clenched fist into the palm of his hand. "Damn me, Page, I believe you have already signed Georgina's death warrant. And to no avail, because Helm is not so stupid as to sit and wait to be attacked by an army. At the first sign of such movement he will be gone, and the situation of the threat to the Prince's safety will remain exactly as before. Georgina's death will be an unnecessary and grievous waste."

Page Cloverly was pale at Pendragon's outburst. "You think I am unfeeling? Do you not realise I would gladly exchange my life for that of Georgina?"

Pendragon softened his voice. "I apologise, Page, forgive me. Of course I realise your feelings; they are no less for Georgina than my own. But at the moment I have a plan that may end the matter. It is a thin plan, but regrettably it is the only one which may work; I must do it alone. I will come with you to Gowers's offices, but I make no promise to obey his orders."

* * *

As if to confirm Pendragon's suspicions that he was under the close surveillance of one of Helm's men, a folded piece of paper had been pushed through the door of the Park Lane house. It was handed to Pendragon by Wolfgang as he brought the men's topcoats and hats. The note was brief. The words may have been Helm's although the writing itself was so accurate in its formation Pendragon guessed it to be that of the more artistic Gaunt. It read 'Remember your commitment'. There was no signature, but equally no doubt of the note's origin.

Pendragon handed the slip of paper to Cloverly. "From Helm! His man will follow us to the palace and undoubtedly wait until he can follow us back. I'm afraid of only one thing, that Helm may have second thoughts of my trustworthiness. If I am to act at all, then it must be soon. Every wasted minute places a greater risk on Georgina's life."

* * *

It was a silent drive to the Palace down Park Lane and then

Constitution Hill between the avenue of tall trees. There was little to discuss, and Pendragon was apprehensive. He had encountered Sir Hubert Gowers in the past, and there was no love lost between them. Gowers was too often stupid and officious.

A Palace guard stopped the coach at the ornate gates, inspected Page Cloverly's credentials, and saluted them through. The coachman swung the carriage across the paved drive and through the arched tunnel beneath the palace to the office area at the building's rear. A groom opened the carriage door and bowed as the two men climbed down. Page Cloverly led the way to Gowers's office, where a lieutenant bade them wait.

It was a dim and frowsty building and the office section was in sad need of repair; the paintwork was flaked and stained. Economy in the palace obviously began in its offices. There was the smell of Government mustiness and beeswax floor polish.

Gowers kept them waiting an unnecessary twenty minutes, and Pendragon knew it was part of the man's way of putting them firmly in their places, even before they met him. At last a spring bell rang behind the lieutenant's desk and he requested them to follow him.

Gowers was not alone. Pendragon was briefly alarmed to find himself confronted by his Queen. He hesitated, and then bowed. Prince Albert stood a little behind her, dwarfing her so that she seemed little more than a child in front of him.

Her eyes were without any hint of warmth. She acknowledged the men's bows with a slight movement of her head. Diminutive she might be, thought Pendragon, but she left no doubt as to her Royal stature.

She glanced at Sir Hubert Gowers. "You may leave us." The request was a firm order. Sir Hubert Gowers frowned at Pendragon, but bowed himself from the room. After he had closed the door the Queen stared unblinking at Pendragon for almost a minute. He felt himself blushing. "We are extremely angry," she said at last; her voice was even colder than her eyes. "Your childish escapade is totally alien to the manner in which we expect our officers to behave. Mister Cloverly has already been told as much. Do you not realise, Captain Pendragon, that your actions, only a few years ago, would have led you to the Tyburn scaffold?"

"Yes, Ma'am," replied Pendragon, keeping his words as brief as was politely possible.

"Only one point is in your favour; it is obvious you are prepared to take any risk, however foolish, to protect my husband. We therefore assume that your loyalty extends also to your Queen."

"Yes, Ma'am."

"Don't yes Ma'am me, Captain Pendragon. We wish to hear, in complete detail, all that has happened to you since the unfortunate and regrettable incident in Piccadilly."

Pendragon told her all. At the mention of the knife blade on Georgina's hand she shuddered. Prince Albert remained silent in the background.

"And that is all?" she asked when Pendragon had finished.

"Yes, Your Majesty."

For the first time, she looked at Prince Albert. He opened his mouth to say something, but she silenced him. "It is quite obvious," she said firmly, "that my dear husband must be removed from the possibility of any attack. He will leave for Scotland today. And you, Captain Pendragon, you presumably have some vague idea as to the whereabouts of these villains?"

"I believe it may be possible for me to find them. There were certain clues, Ma'am," agreed Pendragon.

"Of course there would be certain clues! You are a Queen's Agent, and therefore presumably a man used, though we doubt you are suited, to this kind of work. You will find the place; this is our personal order. You will find it within the next twenty-four hours. Once you have its location, you will report here, directly and only to us. We will decide upon the necessary action then."

110

Page Cloverly spoke for the first time. "Your Majesty. The matter of Miss Georgina Carr?"

The Queen raied her head. "England, and the Empire, Mister Cloverly, is presently ruled by a woman. Have you any doubt we would hesitate to lay down our life in its protection? Of course there is no doubt! Women do not necessarily carry sabres or lances, Mister Cloverly, but that does not imply their unwillingness to die for their country. We have no doubt Miss Carr feels as we feel; she is a gentlewoman of some education, we believe. There is *no* matter, Mister Cloverly, of a Miss Carr."

* * *

It was late afternoon as the coach drew away from the Palace, and the coachman swung the horses left and up the gentle hill towards Hyde Park. Pendragon felt sick and heavy-hearted. He realised that he had perhaps seen Georgina for the last time. All the years of love and friendship, ever since his childhood, were to be unrepeatable memories.

There was no doubt Page Cloverly shared his feelings. He sat slumped back in his seat with his eyes closed. "John," he said eventually. "Believe me, if there could have been any way in which I could have kept the news from the Palace, then I would have done so. But I too suffer from orders, and I am expected to obey them regardless of the cost. God knows, the cost is high enough this time."

Pendragon nodded. "But perhaps there is yet a way of our avoiding payment! "

* * *

Pendragon quit Cloverly's carriage at the corner of Green Street a few yards from the Park Lane House. He pushed open its gate, and was climbing the steps leading to the door when a voice hailed him from the street. A horseman, flushed with hard riding, reined his animal to a halt near the kerbside. "Captain Pendragon?"

"Yes." Pendragon walked down the steps towards the man. "A message. Urgent and private." The man waved an envelope, but instead of climbing down from his horse, he kneed it forward until he was on the sidewalk beside Pendragon. The man appeared to be a groom, or was dressed as such with leather leggings above his boots, and coarse serge trousers. He lacked a top coat and was wearing only a waistcoat with his shirt sleeves rolled above thick forearms. He looked as though he had been unexpectedly called from his stable work. He passed the envelope down to Pendragon, and without waiting for a reply turned his animal and kicked it to a canter, away through the Park Lane traffic.

Pendragon climbed the steps again, tearing open the envelope as he did so. There was a sheet of paper, and writing he did not recognise. It seemed to have been written with urgency, as the writer had failed to dry the ink, which had smeared as he folded the sheet and slid it into the envelope. "Be at your residence at seventy-thirty this evening." It was the second unsigned note of the day, but Pendragon had no doubt that like the other it was an order from Helm.

He slapped the envelope against his hand. Helm! Well, if the cause was by any unfortunate chance lost, at least he would have the satisfaction of personally killing one of Helm's men; with luck, even Helm himself. Whoever was the one to visit him this evening would not leave the house alive.

Ted Blower, neatly dressed for a change, opened the front door for Pendragon. He grinned at him. "Hopes you don't mind, Captain, but with Mister Henry not with us, Wolfgang said I'd best take his place and get some training in house duties." He held out his hand for Pendragon's hat, then balanced on his toes to help him off with his coat. "Blimey, Captain, but you looks down in the mouth. Still feelin' bad, are yer?"

"Bad? Oh, my head . . . no, that's better, Ted."

Henry Cox had been right, Ted Blower had changed a lot over the past eighteen months. Good food and a regular bed had built inches to his height, and thickened his frame towards manhood. Had old Rambolt still been alive, he would have failed to recognise the boy now. It seemed a lifetime since Cox had caught Ted spying on a wounded wagoner in an east end alley.

Rambolt! How would the dead agent, Pendragon's predecessor, have handled the present situation? The situation would never have occurred, Pendragon realised. Rambolt the spy-catcher had deliberately chosen to live a solitary life, so he wouldn't have, didn't have, any commitments or ties. There'd been no one to mourn him when he'd finally ended up in a spice chest with his throat cut. Perhaps Rambolt was the wise one, thought Pendragon. Friends and lovers were pleasant in normal circumstance, but they were too much of a liability for a Queen's Agent. They made him too vulnerable, both physically and emotionally. The future? Pendragon chose not to consider it for a moment.

He walked through to the library and found a large scale Cruchley's map of London and its surrounds. He laid it on the leather-topped table and spread it flat. Somewhere on it was Helm's derelict house. The scale of the map was big enough to show even individual dwellings.

Pendragon sat in front of the map and studied it carefully. "North," Cox had said. "North, by the feeling of it." And Cox was an old cavalryman; with almost thirty years of experience of patrols in unmapped parts of India, he was probably right. Pendragon had met soldiers before who had the same sort of ability, men who always managed to know where they were, even though their officers gave them no hints from their maps. He'd heard them in the Crimea, talking amongst themselves as they sat around cook fires late in the evening, after a hard day in the saddle. "Where are we, Mac?" "Use yer bleedin' brains, boy.

113

We rode norf this morning, for two hours didn't we? Then old 'Arry, he 'as us riding west for a while, then norf again along that bloody ridge. We covered thirty miles, I'd say. Ain't there a river called the Alma, north of where we was yesterday? Well, I'd say we was three or four miles short of the bleedin' river Alma." They'd be right, to within a mile of the map position, and not one would be capable of reading the name of a town on a map, let alone a compass bearing.

North! North of London, somewhere! He traced the route of the North London Railway with his finger. North, but not north-east; north-east was too heavily populated. They'd have had to be far longer in the carriage to clear the heavily populated areas of North Holloway or Newington. The metropolis cleared rapidly however, north and north-west of Portland Town.

And why was it Pendragon had been dropped from the coach behind woods near the derelict house? Why hadn't the carriage driven straight to the main entrance of the grounds? Why not? wondered Pendragon. There had to be a reason. The most likely one, as he had told Cox, was that there was something to be seen from that direction which gave positive identification of the situation of the house; some sort of a landmark. Something Helm expected them to know, or to remember.

A landmark! Pendragon opened the desk drawer and found a magnifying glass. He held it over the map and studied the details slowly. A full hour's drive in a coach, it had been. A coach, with sound horses, would make near eight miles an hour at a trot. Allowing for the fact that the driver would most likely take an indirect route, it would place them some five miles from the exit of the Holy Land. Pendragon measured distance with his thumb. There had been a mile of unmade road before the coach had stopped. A landmark, some five miles north, or west of the Holy Land, and with a mile or so of unmade road before it. Porto Bello Farm? Pendragon scoured the area with his magnifying glass. There were no landmarks shown. He checked the

114

distance again. Porto Bello was probably too far west. He examined the area north of the Albert Park; it was again heavily populated.

The Shoot Up Hill windmill! He bit his lip; it was a possibility. He found an inch rule and made the measurement carefully. Five and a quarter miles from Holy Land; easily extended to seven or eight miles, if a coachman was to take the less direct route through the side streets bordering Grove Road and Maida Hill. The Shoot Up Hill windmill was a landmark Helm would expect any Londoner who owned a carriage to recognise; it was a popular Sunday picnic spot! Woods? There were plenty to the south of the windmill. He studied the map until his headache returned and his eyes watered with the strain of concentration. There was a link road, little more than a bridlepath, between Wilsdon Green and the Edgware Road; it was unmetalled, merely a flint track. There were woods on either side of the narrow road, and in one section of woods was an open piece of ground and the pin-point mark of a house. A thin dotted line, so faint as to be almost indiscernible to the naked eye, ran from the minute black dot to the edge of the open piece of ground. The drive to the house! From the map it was obvious that if a man were to stand at the point where the drive touched the main Edgware Road he would be in direct line with the Shoot Up Hill windmill; the landmark Helm sought to hide! Pendragon was certain he was right.

He studied the map for a further hour, checking any other possible alternatives; there were none. It *had* to be Helm's lair.

* * *

It was autumn dusk. Pendragon sat at the library desk and stared out of the window. Below was the stable yard and he could hear the groom and coachman chatting as they fed the horses. In the kitchen one of the housemaids laughed as the groom called a saucy remark to her through the window; there was a clattering of dishes. Outwardly it was a normal evening, but Pendragon knew that evenings in the Park Lane House might never be the same again. He felt as though he were being torn apart by his loyalties. Georgina's life, or at least a chance to save it, against a direct order from his Queen.

"Damn . . . damn!" Perhaps there had been too many years of discipline for them to be easily cast aside now.

The visitor! Pendragon remembered the note. The man could arrive at any time. He jerked himself to his feet and hurried up the stairs, two at a time, to his bedroom. He paused briefly to light the gas lamp, and opened the door of his wardrobe. His military dress uniform, now only a souvenir smelling of camphor, hung in front of him. He pushed it aside. His sabre stood against the far corner of the wardrobe. He lifted it out and reached for a mahogany box on the shelf. He tossed the sabre on to his bed and opened the box; it was fitted for a brace of large holster pistols, but contained only one of the pair. The other had been lost somewhere during that terrible charge at Balaclava and was probably still buried in the Crimean mud.

Pendragon removed the remaining pistol from its case. It was a heavy, double-barrelled Westley Richards, a ten-bore capable of knocking a man clean from his horse if the ball hit him fair and square. The type had been a favourite with young army officers who had nicknamed the weapons 'infidel killers', because of their ability to drop even drug-crazed Dervishes dead in their tracks. Pendragon pulled out the ramrod and slid it down the barrel, measuring the slim rod of wood against the barrel length. The pistol was unloaded, so he charged both barrels with powder and followed up the charge with a pair of wadded lead balls. He checked the trigger actions, lowering the hammers carefully with his thumb, lifted them again and primed the nipples with percussion caps. The pistol was ready for use. He jammed it into his waistband; it felt clumsy and uncomfortable compared with the more modern weapon Helm had taken from him.

He picked up his sabre from the bed and shook the scabbard from the blade. It gleamed like dull gold in the gas light and was familiar and comforting to his hand.

Damn Helm! Pendragon would have given everything he owned to have the murderer in front of him now. Pendragon swore aloud. He would seek out Helm, orders or not! It would be impossible to live with himself if he permitted the swine to kill Georgina without making any attempt at saving her life. There might be dishonour at disobeying his Sovereign's orders, perhaps even disgrace and exile, but at least it would all happen with his conscience clear. He felt his heart lightening and a sudden flush of excitement at the thought.

He would wait until Helm's man arrived, kill him, and then go after the others. His prime objective was to get Georgina and Cox from their hands. Once they were freed, then and only then, would he make his report; the Army could do what they pleased! He felt happier. He chuckled and swung the sabre at an invisible adversary.

* * *

The doorbell rang, its high-pitched jingling cutting into Pendragon's thoughts. He stopped the movement of the sabre in mid-swing, his face serious. He waited and heard Ted Blower answer the bell. There was the mutter of voices and the sound of the drawing room door closing. Ted Blower's boots clumped on the stairs and stopped outside Pendragon's bedroom. There was a light knock, and Ted Blower's voice.

"Captain, Sir. A visitor, Captain."

Pendragon opened the door. "A man, or a gentleman?" he asked. God grant it would be Helm.

Ted Blower thought for a moment. "I'd think a gentleman, Captain, by his clothes. A well-built man, and tall. Didn't get a proper look at his face as he wouldn't take his hat off . . . that's why I weren't certain he was a gent."

"Helm it is," breathed Pendragon with satisfaction. It was almost too good to be true. Helm, here in the house! There were only two ways in which the man would leave; manacled and chained to a well-armed police officer, or dead! "Ted, listen carefully and do as I say. The man downstairs is dangerous. Keep well away from the door after I enter. Don't make a move unless I call you. If it sounds like a fight, or if you hear a shot, then wait and see if I appear. If I do not, then go for the police as fast as you can. Understand?"

"Blimey, Captain, yes," said Ted. His eyes glistened excitedly. "You been up to a bit of the old Rambolt, then, Captain? Cor, wish you'd let me in on it!"

"You may be in yet," warned Pendragon. "Now remember what I've said." He handed the boy the sabre. "Put this somewhere handy outside in the hall."

He walked slowly down the wide stairs and paused in front of the drawing-room door. He slid his hand beneath his jacket, drew out the heavy pistol and thumbed back the hammers. He braced himself and opened the door softly.

* * *

A man, broad-shouldered, and with his topcoat collar turned high around his neck, sat in one of the armchairs facing the fire with his back towards Pendragon. The man's head rested on his hands. He was staring into the blazing coals like a gypsy fortune teller. His tall hat was on the floor beside him.

Pendragon moved silently until he was only six feet from the man. Then he spoke. "If you move, I will kill you."

The figure in the armchair jerked slightly, but said nothing.

"Lift your hands away from your body so I can see them," ordered Pendragon. "And do it slowly and with great care. My pistol has hair triggers."

The man obeyed, but now spoke. "I find this an interesting although unexpected situation," he said calmly. His accent was

118

terrifyingly familiar. "May I turn to face you?" He did not wait for Pendragon to reply, but eased himself confidently from the chair and turned.

"Oh, good God!" gasped Pendragon. He lowered the pistol.

Prince Albert chuckled as though he were witnessing a successful practical joke. "For one moment, Captain Pendragon, I really thought you had joined forces with the assassins! Your method of greeting me is quite original."

* * *

For several seconds Pendragon stood, feeling increasingly foolish, with the heavy pistol dangling at his side. He swallowed and half bowed, awkwardly. "Your Highness, Sir. I offer my sincere..."

"No, Captain Pendragon," grinned Prince Albert. "Your apologies are not required. Perhaps it is I who should apologise; after all, I gave you no indication in my letter whom you should expect." He took two steps towards Pendragon and stopped close in front of him. "Captain," he said urgently, but with his eyes twinkling. "First your word, as one of my officers, a gentleman, and, I trust, a friend. Your complete silence as to my presence here tonight. I am, as you might say, incognito. I am, in fact, halfway to Scotland now, asleep in the Royal railway carriage." He laughed. "I am the naughty boy who was sent to bed early, but who has escaped through the bedroom window."

"But, Sir, you'll be missed. There will be a great hue and cry."

Prince Albert shook his head. "No, I will not be missed. I am second only to one other in the realm, and still, I believe, have a little influence, if only amongst my own servants. It is arranged that I am to appear to be ill at York. I, or rather the other me, will leave the train there, well wrapped in blankets. Her Majesty will be informed by telegram that I intend to rest, until I am fully recovered, at the Regal Arms Spa. I think, Captain

119

Pendragon, I have at least a full twenty-four hours before discovery is likely. Long before then I hope to be in York, in person."

"Well, I . . ." began Pendragon. At the moment he could not imagine the reason for the Prince's visit. He took a deep breath. "A brandy, Sir?"

"That's better, Captain." The Prince swung off his top coat and tossed it across the back of a chair. He turned and stood with his back to the fire, his hands clasped behind him.

Pendragon uncocked the pistol, laid it on a side table and rang the servant's bell. Even before it finished ringing, the door of the drawing room burst open and a wild-eyed Ted Blower hurtled into the room, waving Pendragon's sabre in front of him like some demented and clumsy warrior. Pendragon, although startled by the boy's sudden entrance, dived at him and caught him in mid-stride, his sabre already raised to swing a cut at the visitor. Pendragon spun him round on his feet, wrenched the sabre from his hand, and, in one movement, cracked the flat of the blade across the boy's backside. "You young idiot," he roared angrily.

"Yes, Captain, Sir," gulped Ted Blower, his feet barely touching the ground as Pendragon hoisted him towards the door by his collar.

"Now go and get the brandy, boy. And see if you can bring it in with a little more decorum than you showed this time. Don't you recognise our visitor?"

"Yes, Sir. I knows him now." Ted's voice was a warble.

"Then say nothing to the household, ruffian. This is Her Majesty's business; keep your mouth closed." Pendragon began mentally preparing yet another apology for the Prince, but the man was laughing, laughing so heartily that tears ran down his cheeks.

He dabbed at his eyes with a kerchief. "Captain Pendragon, this is capital, really capital. I assure you in my dull life there is

120

little to equal your splendid entertainments. Tell me, Captain, is your life always so exciting in Park Lane, or have I managed to catch you on the night of a gala performance?"

* * *

A few minutes later, Ted Blower appeared with the brandy decanter and glasses. He kept his head down and was blushing so furiously the back of his neck was a bright scarlet. As he left the room he risked a glance at Pendragon, who scowled theatrically at him. The boy shut the door silently. Pendragon poured the brandy and passed a glass to the Prince.

Prince Albert sipped the liquid. He was serious now. "I imagine, Captain Pendragon, you are wondering why I am here." Pendragon nodded. "A simple matter of honour, Captain. Ladies, I fear, do not always view honour in the same light as we gentlemen. I am here, Captain Pendragon, because of your aunt, Miss Carr." He turned his back on Pendragon and stared down into the fire again.

Some moments passed before he spoke again. "What has your aunt told you of our past relationship, Captain Pendragon?"

"Why, nothing, Sir."

"Nothing, ever?"

"No, Sir."

"No," said the Prince, softly. "She would say nothing. It is how I knew it would be." He faced Pendragon again, looking him straight in the eyes. "I rely on your total discretion in the matter, Captain, but it is right you should now know. Your aunt and I, Captain . . . we were in love, in love as only two young and innocent people can be. It was a long time ago, while I was still a student, at first in Italy, then Bonn and Brussels. A lifetime ago; so long ago that I sometimes wonder if it were not two different people. Then I married. I told Prince Wilhelm it should not be so, but one has one's commitments and duties. Do not think, Captain Pendragon, that this is a criticism of my wife, your

121

Queen; I love her very dearly. I do not have any regrets. However, it is necessary you know this little history as an indication of my present feelings of honour. Despite what was said this afternoon at your interview with Her Majesty, I will not and I cannot allow the death of Miss Carr, without doing everything possible in my power to prevent it. I am here, Captain Pendragon, to rescind my wife's directive to you. If there are to be repercussions, then they will be on my head and not on yours. I hope there will be none, but in that unhappy event you may rest assured I will take the full responsibility. I am here, Captain Pendragon, to *order* you personally to save Miss Carr's life, if it is humanly possible to do so. Furthermore, it is my intention to assist you." He paused, and smiled grimly at Pendragon. "If I know you, and I believe I am beginning to do so, then I imagine my order to you is unnecessary; no doubt, Captain Pendragon, you already had something in mind."

Pendragon's thoughts were kaleidoscopic. Brief words, long forgotten conversations and remarks flashed through his mind. He could even remember some comment which had brought instant rebuke to his late guardian; something about Georgina's ankle having turned the head of a German prince! It had been years before, in his childhood, even before he had met his beautiful aunt. The background of her household, with its unusual complement of German staff, and her mysterious pension, was now clear and understandable; as also, was the way Georgina clung to the existence of a gay spinster when she could have taken the hands of a hundred titled men in London's society. She had kept her secret so well, he realised he could have continued to live in her house for another ten years without it becoming known to him. It was a confidence he determined never to break.

The Prince's voice cut into his thoughts. "Have I lost you, Captain? You have been standing silent for a full minute!" Prince Albert spoke gently, understanding that his admission had confused Pendragon. "I asked you, Captain, if you had something already planned?"

* * *

Pendragon now felt relieved. Prince Albert's order to try to save Georgina removed the guilt of his intention to disobey the Queen's direct orders. He was, however, nervous of Prince Albert's mention of personal assistance.

"I have had one idea," he said at last. "I believe I have found the whereabouts of Helm's hideout. I have studied a large-scale map of London and I think, from what little information Cox and myself learned on our route there, that the house is near the Shoot Up Hill windmill. I've spent some time this afternoon considering various possibilities regarding the place, and I had decided I would try to get into the building on my own."

"Not very easy, Captain, if I remember correctly your description of Mister Helm's leopards. I say *Mister* Helm, you will note, Captain, because my extremely thorough wife, this very afternoon, gave instructions to the Herald's Office that Helm's title and any honours were to be struck from the records. A singular and thorough woman, Queen Victoria," he mused. "Continue, Captain."

"Once inside, I was determined to account for as many of Helm's men as I could manage. I planned throat-cutting and silent murder, rather than chivalry."

"Throat-cutting and silent murder sounds excellent and appropriate, Captain." Prince Albert spoke with a harshness that was uncharacteristic. "But tell me, how did you plan to pass the four leopards?"

"I had thought of ammonia," replied Pendragon. "You will remember how when Cox and I tried to escape, using one of Helm's men's clothing, the leopards were puzzled and didn't attack? Well, it occurred to me that if scent was so important to them I could disguise all smell by dousing my clothing with

123

ammonia. It's extremely pungent and I was counting on it confusing them long enough for me to get to the house."

"And if it failed?"

"My sabre! I've watched how they dash in for an attack, and with luck I would account for a couple of the beasts; they are not always around together. I decided I couldn't risk a gun shot, it would be bound to arouse guards."

"And you were going to do this alone? You are quite mad, Captain!" Prince Albert sighed. "If you were still a serving officer, I fear you would be either a General or a corpse by this time. Don't remind me, Captain, I am aware of the dash, cut, thrust and retreat tactics of my hussars. They are seldom, however, concerned with packs of man-eating leopards. Tell me, you were planning to do this on foot, no doubt?"

"Yes, Sir."

Prince Albert shook his head sadly. "You would never have made General, Captain Pendragon. Show me your map."

Pendragon fetched it from the library. He was finding the Prince an enigma. The man's reputation was one of shyness, with few leanings towards military tactics, and yet, from the way he was talking, he had a keen and ready mind. His shyness was obviously a public mask.

He handed the map to the Prince who unfolded it on the floor in front of him, then got down on to his knees to make a closer examination. "Here," said Pendragon, putting his finger on the small dot that indicated Helm's derelict house and its ranging grounds.

The Prince studied the map for a few minutes. "How high are the walls around the grounds?"

"About ten feet," answered Pendragon.

"Then what keeps the leopards inside?" asked the Prince. "In my biological gardens I am assured sixteen feet is the minimum height for a leopard's cage, as well as a strong roof on top."

"Iron spikes on the inside of the walls. They are fixed on the inner lip at the top of the wall and extend some four feet inwards and downwards, like the mouth of a lobster pot. Any animal trying to leap the wall would be impaled, and if it tried to scramble the ten feet of brickwork it would meet an apparently impenetrable barrier of steel bars near the top."

"I see," mused Prince Albert. He paused for a few moments in thought. "Pendragon, have you considered how foolish my hussars would appear if they were to make charges in battle, on foot, as infantrymen? They are quite wrongly equipped for the purpose; wrongly equipped, wrongly armed, and wrongly trained. A hussar is lost without his horse. Is that not so, Captain Pendragon?"

"Quite true, Sir."

"Good, Captain Pendragon. Then consider my notion; I suggest the attack is made by horse. True, it will not be quite as silent as on foot, but there is far more chance of success. You would have speed and surprise on your side, which is the expectation of cavalry. The ground inside the walls is probably soft; it has been a wet autumn. Hoof beats will not be very loud, and the ear often fails to hear unaccustomed sounds."

"The walls, Sir," reminded Pendragon. "I know of no horse capable of a leap of ten feet."

"My own hunter has leapt over six feet," said Prince Albert. "Ten feet is but four more than that. If it could clear the wall on the outside with a jump of less than ten, then the full ten-foot drop on the inside would be well within the capabilities of a sound and willing horse. We need a four-foot platform on to which the horses could be galloped." He flicked his finger tips. "Quick now, Captain, give me an idea . . ."

Pendragon's mind raced. He was aware the Prince was ahead of him with his thoughts. "A hay wain, Sir," he said.

"Excellent, Captain. A hay wain. A good sized hay wagon from a nearby farm. That would be even higher than four feet."

125

"Nearer five, I'd say, Sir. But it wouldn't be easy for a horse. The two jumps would have to be made almost simultaneously, one on to the hay wain, and then a second over the wall."

"But if it were an excellent animal, and wasn't expecting the jumps, it would make them if it were spurred. If it were a defence to a redoubt then you would try it, eh, Captain?"

Pendragon nodded. "Yes, I would try it."

"Leading your troop?"

"With my troop."

"Then you would consider it a chance, Captain, in the heat of a battle?"

"Yes, it would be a chance worth taking. By God, Sir, yes."

"And so, Captain, we have overcome the first hurdle; the wall." Prince Albert grinned again like a schoolboy planning a raid on a farmer's orchard. "The leopards, Captain; they do not seem quite so harmful when viewed from the back of a horse. How are you with a lance?"

"Rusty," admitted Pendragon. "But I was brought up to one, in my father's regiment in India."

"So, we have two men, on good horses, both with lances, and with sabres." The Prince rubbed his hands together. "I would rather be a man on a horse with a lance than a leopard on the ground. It is the finest field sport, Captain, hunting with a lance. I took part in many such hunts against our German wild boar in my youth. Your British foxes and deer are far too tame."

Pendragon felt uncomfortable. "Sir, you must forgive me, but I really cannot let you risk your life in this way. I beg you to allow me to do this alone! If you insist I do it in company, then I have friends in the Guards and Cavalry Club who would be willing to assist me. If you were to lose your life in this venture, then it would be no different to the assassin's bullet."

Prince Albert took hold of Pendragon's arm, his fingers biting into the firm muscles. "Captain," he said fiercely, "one

126

person only in the whole world forbids me anything, and you are not that person. From the time I made up my mind to involve myself in this matter I have known my life was at risk. There is a letter in the hands of one of my servants to that effect. I have given you my reasons, Captain Pendragon. I demand you honour them."

"Very well, Sir," said Pendragon glumly.

Prince Albert pushed himself up and sat in the chair again. He ran his fingertips along his moustache. "And what other problems are there to be solved?"

"I fear you are touching it, Sir. Your moustache, Sir. If you are determined to accompany me then I suggest you must disguise yourself a little. Your Highness's face is familiar to every Londoner, but the removal of your moustache and a little shortening of your sideburns would render the dangers of recognition less likely."

"You think it important? Yes, I see that it is so!" He touched his moustache again. "A sacrifice, Captain. I agree with you, it must come off. I shall beg the use of your razor. And anything else, Captain, besides my appearance?"

"Our only immediate problems are good horses and weapons. My own pistol is an unusual size and I am short of ball; we'll be better off with standard cavalry models. There is also the difficulty of leaving this house unobserved by Helm's spies," said Pendragon. "This house is being watched, Sir, and the watchers will already know I have a visitor. Thank God, though, they do not know your identity. However, we must leave the house by some manner other than the normal method. It's a pity, for I would like to have ridden my own charger, Dasher Charlie. He has courage enough for the jump."

"Mounts and weapons are easily arranged, Captain. There are several barracks within a couple of miles of here."

"As it is imperative to maintain your anonymity, Sir, I believe I should make those arrangements for us," Pendragon advised.

"I have friends in the regiments, and they know me well enough not to question my motives or reasons." He rang the servant's bell again. A few seconds later Ted Blower appeared, this time more composed, although still sheepish. "Ted," Pendragon made his voice serious. "I've a little of Rambolt's work for you to do."

Ted's face brightened to a wide grin. "Yes, Captain."

"Can you get out of this house unobserved by anyone who may be watching outside?"

"Bet on my life, Captain. Across the stable roof and down into Wood's Mews." The boy fidgeted with enthusiasm.

"Good. Then get away as fast as you can manage. Go first to the Guards and Cavalry Club in Pall Mall; you'll have to do it at a run as we have little time. When you get there, ask for Lieutenant Beauchamp of the Dragoon Guards. If he's there, and he usually is at this time, then tell him I need the two best hunters he can lay his hands on. I need them in two hours' time. He is to have them waiting in the trees at the Tyburn site. I also want two strong war lances—not ceremonial ones—a brace of pistols, powder and shot, and two other-ranks' swords. As far as the swords are concerned I'd prefer Heavy Dragoon patterns with a bit of weight to them. And if Lieutenant Beauchamp is not at the Guards and Cavalry, then try the Knightsbridge Barracks. Can you remember all that?"

"Two good 'unters, war lances, pistols and ammunition. Heavy Dragoon sabres," repeated the boy, counting the items on his fingers.

"The best hunters, Ted. Those known as good at the jumps."

"Very well, Captain."

"By nine-thirty at the Tyburn copse."

"Yes, Captain."

"Then be off with you."

The boy grinned again, and left them.

128

Prince Albert looked at Pendragon. "Is the lad as reliable as he's keen?"

"He's the boy who spent four years with Rambolt the old spy-catcher," replied Pendragon. "He was watching when Rambolt was killed. I know of no one else as trustworthy."

* * *

An hour and a half later, the two men left the house by the same route as Ted Blower. There was a little consternation in the kitchen as the men passed through, but Pendragon warned the staff to remain silent about the matter, and to stay indoors despite anything that might happen. There was little possibility of anyone recognising Prince Albert now. He had removed his stiff collar and cravat in favour of a loose scarf to give him easier movement, and he was bareheaded. The loss of his moustache and sideburns made his face younger and chubbier.

Once in Wood's Mews Pendragon paused and strapped on his spurs. Prince Albert did likewise. "Everything well, Sir?" asked Pendragon.

Prince Albert, a tall and burly shadow in the near darkness, nodded. "It's a long time since I did any such climbing, Captain. I'm a little out of practice, perhaps." He rubbed his hands, now soot-blackened, against his trousers. "The sight of me so dirty might surprise a few of my associates."

Pendragon led the way out into Park Lane and crossed the road to the trees bordering the park. There were a few pedestrians taking the evening air, and one or two private carriages on the road. A little way down Park Lane stood a rank of Hackneys but Pendragon ignored them, taking a diagonal route northwards to bring them to the small copse a few yards below the old Tyburn gallows site.

They reached the copse. A sudden movement in the shadow of one of the thick beech trees startled Pendragon, but whispered and panting encouragement in a female voice indicated it was probably only a prostitute and her client. Apart from the couple, the copse was empty.

* * *

The evening air was damp. Pendragon shivered and pulled out his pocket watch; it was now two hours since Ted Blower had been sent on his errand. Pendragon swore silently. It was possible the boy had been unable to find Beauchamp. It might have been wiser for the men to wait at the house until he arrived back from his errand.

Prince Albert was also obviously feeling the cold night air. He banged his arms together like a night watchman before his fire on a winter's night, and stamped his feet to restore the circulation.

There was the distant sound of hoof beats on the soft ground. Pendragon stared hopefully into the darkness. The hoofbeats came nearer until at last Pendragon could see two horsemen, one of them leading a riderless horse, silhouetted against the night sky. He waited until they were within a few yards before stepping from the shadow of the trees.

The horsemen pulled their mounts to a halt. "Pendragon?"

"Beechy!"

"Damn me, yes, Pendragon. Along with your shipping order. Gad, I don't know what you're up to 'Dragon, but sure as hell I'm not missing out." Young Lieutenant Beauchamp was as bubbly as ever, raring for any form of action to relieve the boredom of peacetime soldiering in the Metropolis. "Two good horses, your lad said, and damn me I've stolen the best in the barracks. I say," he chuckled, "one of the dashed beasts belongs to old Colonel Fat Arse himself. He'd have me flayed alive if he found out. It's the bay. Got your weapons, too, though stab me if I know what you want those clumsy sabres for. Could have got some jolly pretty ones from the mess display. I say, 'Dragon, what a lark old Fitzpatrick isn't in on this, or Lumley. Drat me, that isn't one of 'em in the shadows, is it? Thought I'd be one up on the fellows. I say, it's not old Fitz, is it?"

Pendragon chuckled. "No, Beechy, it's not Fitz, but I'm afraid you're not coming along with us. It's strictly a private affair."

"Oh, damn it all," groaned Beauchamp. "Look here, 'Dragon old fellow, I don't jolly well enjoy being treated as your blasted Quartermaster. I've risked my commission with these dashed animals. Could easily find myself hauled across the hot coals for it and lose seniority. I mean, well, dash it, I did a pretty good job last time, didn't I? Not a coward or anything?"

Pendragon laughed. "No, Beechy, not a coward."

"The Lieutenant might prove himself useful, don't you think, Captain?" suggested Prince Albert. "An extra man might well be of use to us in our preparations at the wall."

Beauchamp's keen ears identified the Prince's voice, although until now he had taken little notice of the man. "Oh, good Lord," he exclaimed. "Here, 'Dragon, don't I know that dashed accent? The Regimental dinner a week ago . . . 'Dragon, it's not, is it?" The Prince stepped out of the darkness. Beauchamp peered at him. "You've cut your . . . oh, good Lord." He stiffened on his horse and saluted furiously. "Dashed sorry old . . . er, Your Highness. Didn't mean accent, meant . . . er, oh God!" He saluted again.

"My wife tells me my accent is part of my charm," said Prince Albert warmly. "Well, Captain Pendragon?"

"He could help outside the wall, Sir," agreed Pendragon, emphasising the word 'outside'. He remembered the last occasion he had been helped by the young Lieutenant. Beauchamp was always enthusiastic, but with the fire of his lack of years he was more often in scrapes than out of them. He had the knack of acting without giving matters much thought, until it was too late and he was neck deep in trouble.

"Hurrah!" exclaimed Beauchamp loudly.

"Be quiet, or I'll change my mind," warned Pendragon. "Do you have the lances and pistols?"

"Pistols in saddle holsters, and the lances strapped together on the bay. Too conspicuous to just carry the damned things. What in heavens do you plan with lances, old boy? By the way, the pistols are loaded and there's more powder and balls in the pouches."

Ted Blower had been silent in the saddle of the bay hunter. Now he dismounted. "Do you want me with you too, Captain, Sir?"

"No thanks, Ted. You've done your job for tonight. Get off home. And go in the same way as you got out."

"Right, Captain. Oh, and good luck." He turned and jogged away into the darkness.

"Take your pick, Sir," said Pendragon to the Prince, indicating the horses. Prince Albert took the reins of Beauchamp's Colonel's bay, wedged his foot in a stirrup, and pulled himself into the saddle.

* * *

It took half an hour for the riders to reach Kilburn. The route was direct enough; straight up the Edgware Road from the point where Beauchamp had met them with the horses. The districts changed in character as they drew away from the better residential area above Hyde Park. At first the road was wide, passing through several well-planned and attractive squares surrounded by good quality houses. It then narrowed, lined with dwellings of a more meagre type. There were soon no street lights other than those hanging outside the few inns and taverns on the main north road. The districts were quite different from those in the city and east end of London, where gin and ale houses would have been evident every few hundred yards.

Once Pendragon had explained the purpose of their outing to Beauchamp, and warned him that if he were ever to mention

132

word of the Prince's involvement he would bring eternal wrath and disgrace on his head, the men rode silently. The built-up area of London gradually thinned out until there were houses only on the right hand side of the road, and fields to the left. Beyond Kilburn Well the houses ended, apart from those of farms or small communities of farm workers. The workers, being early risers, were already asleep, and the only sound of habitation was the occasional barking or yapping of their dogs, or the clatter of geese in garden pens.

By half past ten the men had reached the cut-off at Mapes Lane, and turned left there. Pendragon had the comforting feeling he was on the correct route. Although he had seen little from the smoked glass windows of Helm's coach, there was a familiarity he hoped was not merely optimism. They passed Brondesbury House and Pendragon remembered an occasion some years before, when he had gone there with Georgina for a coming-out ball for a friend's daughter. It seemed a lifetime ago; he couldn't even remember the girl's name. She had been a silly little thing, he had thought at the time, but he could only have been seventeen himself then and she was probably a well married and perhaps a beautiful woman by now.

After another half a mile he led them into Walm Lane. There was a darkened farm building on the corner. Beyond, woods thickened along the roadside. Several hundred yards farther along the narrow lane Pendragon paused and drew his horse on to the grass verge.

"Sir, this is it!"

"The house?"

"The track, Sir. Off here, going into the woods on our right."

"Are you certain, Captain?"

"Almost positive," replied Pendragon. "If you'll remain here, I'll make sure I'm right." He pulled his horse into the wood and kneed it to a trot. There was moonlight, thin and pale as a slim crescent lifted above the bank of cloud on the horizon. It was enough, now Pendragon's eyes had fully adjusted to the darkness, to enable him to see the track ahead of his animal. He reached a gate, leant and opened it, barging it clear with his horse's shoulder. The ground at the side of the track was ploughed, with deep woods away to his left. He crossed the field and passed a second gate leading again into thicker woodland. The moon seemed to dim. A thick shadow loomed ahead. The wall and a narrow gateway! Pendragon slid from his horse and moved cautiously forward to the gate. It was worth trying; there was always the chance it was unlocked. He pressed against it, but it refused to move. He remounted and turned his horse, walking it away until he was sure he was far enough from the grounds for the hoof beats to remain unheard before he urged it to a canter.

He seemed to reach the lane quicker on his return journey. Prince Albert and Beauchamp stood by their horses under the overhanging hedges.

"Well?"

"It's the place, all right. I checked the gate, but it was bolted. We have to jump the wall. We need the hay cart now."

"If you'll excuse me," said Beauchamp, blandly. "I was wondering about that, 'Dragon. Where the hades does one find a hay wain in the middle of the damned night?"

"At a farm," Prince Albert answered, as if the hiring of hay wains at midnight was a common occurrence.

"Yes, of course, Sir." Beauchamp had obviously decided against questioning anything the Prince said.

"The farm cottage we passed at the corner," suggested Pendragon. "They're bound to have one, or know of one."

"Dear fellow," Beauchamp spoke in a bored tone of voice. "Don't you imagine they'll think us just a little eccentric? I mean to say, well, actually, not too many of our sort of fellows are likely to have such needs."

"Money buys anything," said Pendragon with conviction. He

dug his heels into his horse's side and led the way back down the lane.

* * *

The cottage was dark and silent as Pendragon swung himself from his saddle and handed his reins to Beauchamp. Beauchamp was grinning, his teeth showing in the moonlight. "I say, 'Dragon, jolly good luck."

Pendragon walked up the narrow path to the cottage door. He banged on the heavy oak door with his fist. There was sudden barking inside, then someone swore at the dog and there was silence again. Pendragon repeated his knock and the dog snarled.

"Go to buggery," shouted a voice inside the cottage.

"I'd like a few words with you," called Pendragon.

"Piss off, whoever you are," answered the voice, angrily. The dog barked again, snarling and scratching at the inside of the door.

"We want to hire a cart," said Pendragon. Behind him, Beauchamp laughed at Pendragon's obvious discomfort.

"I don't bloody well hire carts," shouted the voice from inside the cottage. "Now beetle away, whoever you are, before I puts a load of rough shot up your breeches. Pissing around disturbin' workin' folk in the . . ." The voice died to a threatening grumble.

Beauchamp joined Pendragon at the door. He hammered it with the hilt of his sword. The dog's barking became shrill with fury. "You in there, I say," yelled Beauchamp. "Fellow, your damned thatch is on fire."

"Right," growled the voice inside. "That does it. If one of yer gets killed now, it's yer own bleedin' fault." There were sounds of fumbling. A wooden shutter a few yards along the side of the cottage was thrust open.

Pendragon pushed Beauchamp back into the doorway out of line of the man's gun muzzle.

135

"I say, fellow," called Beauchamp. "I wasn't joking about the thatch. See here." A match flared in his hand. No sooner had it sparked to life than there was an explosion at the window and the whistle of buckshot past the two men's faces.

"You damned idiot, Beechy," swore Pendragon, knocking the burning match from Beauchamp's fingers.

"Piss off, I says," roared the man at the window. "Next shot'll blow yer heads off."

"He doesn't scare easily." Beauchamp sounded surprised. "I say, fellow. What would you rather have, ten guineas or no roof to your cottage?"

"Ten guineas?" said the voice, still angrily but with some curiosity. "Ten guineas! Don't make me bloody laugh." The man was at least listening.

"Ten guineas for the loan of your hay cart; that's probably more than it's worth," said Pendragon quickly. There was a chance now the man was calmer. "I've a friend hurt; he fell from his horse a mile up the road. We have to get him to an inn. We need a cart badly and we'll pay ten guineas."

"Ten?" asked the man's voice. "With or without an 'orse?"

"With a horse, at that price," answered Pendragon. "We've only riding animals of our own. For God's sake, our companion is dying."

"Make it twelve and you can keep the damn'd horse and cart," said the man at the window. "Pass your money here, as I ain't comin' out. And don't try nothing as me gun's loaded again and'll be pointing at you. Just come 'ere with the ready." The man was still half angry and disbelieving.

Pendragon moved cautiously along the side of the cottage. He found his wallet and slid twelve gold coins from the narrow coin pouch.

"Count 'em on to the windy ledge," said the man. Pendragon did so. There was the clink of coins as the man took them, weighed them in his hand and examined them. "Jesus Christ! It bloody *is* twelve guineas! Jesus!"

The money, Pendragon realised, was probably more cash than the man had ever held in his hands before. "Where are they, then?"

"The 'orse and cart, Mister?" The man was so interested in the money he'd forgotten his reason for having it. "The cart? Christ, yes, Mister! It's round the back in me yard." The man's attitude had changed. "I'm sorry, Mister, it ain't a good cart but it'll suffice, no doubt. You'll be wanting harness, and that's in the shed with the horse." He paused. "Mister, I forgot the harness! It'll be a little more, I'd think."

"Another guinea?"

"God, yes, Mister! Another guinea, that'd be most fair."

Pendragon passed him the final gold coin. "Come on round the back and help," he told Beauchamp.

The man at the window began pulling the shutter closed. There was no doubt he could hardly as yet believe his luck, but was taking no chances that the coin might yet be stolen back from him by his midnight visitors.

"Hey!" Beauchamp took hold of the shutter and leant forward. "I say, fellow," he said confidentially. "Don't you know that if by chance, tomorrow morning, you were to take a stroll in those woods a mile up the road from here, where the path goes off to the right, there's just a chance you might get your dashed old hay cart back again." The man at the window, his face lit by the moonlight, looked at him in astonishment. "Ta ta, old man." Beauchamp pushed the shutter closed.

* * *

Harnessing an unfamiliar horse to cart shafts was more difficult than Pendragon had anticipated. The shafts were splintered, warped and rough, and built for a horse of far greater girth than the half-starved animal they found in the stable. The harness

137

was also in poor condition, old and badly repaired, and resembled in no way the type of harness Pendragon had seen used on the field artillery guns and limbers. It took them a noisy half hour to get the animal into position, and Beauchamp collected a bruised face from the horse's head as it refused time and again to allow him to fasten the straw-stuffed collar about its neck. Once in the harness and between the shafts the animal sulked like a temperamental mule and had to be brutally encouraged before it would take even a step. At last, groaning and panting as though it were in its final agony, the animal jerked forward and drew the creaking hay wain from the yard.

Beauchamp, his charger tied ignominiously, he felt, to the hay wain's tailboard, sat uncomfortably on the seat of the wagon, with the reins in his hands and the corners of his mouth turned down like some child suffering unjust punishment. They reached the track leading to Helm's estate before he spoke, and then it was only an encouragement to the animal. As they neared the wall, however, he brightened again. "I say, 'Dragon," he called.

Pendragon hushed him. "For God's sake, man. We want silence now. Draw the cart alongside the wall, and then stop."

Beauchamp did so. Pendragon dismounted, climbed on to the back of the cart, and then on to the seat beside Beauchamp. "A leg-up," he hissed. Beauchamp made a cup from his hands and Pendragon stood in it and reached upwards until he could see over the wall. Below were a group of bushes that made it quite impossible for a horse to land safely on the other side. A little to his left, however, he could see a short clearing some twenty yards in length. He slid down from the wall. "Pull ahead a little way." Beauchamp shook the reins, clicked with his tongue, and the animal moved forward again with a groan. Pendragon clambered the wall a second time. There was a clear space in front of him. He looked for the leopards but could see no sign of them. He climbed down.

There was a soft voice from the side of the cart. "How is it?" asked the Prince.

"A clear space for landing. Do you want a look at it?"

"No. I think I'd rather take the wall blind. It is more difficult to fear that which you can't see."

"What now, 'Dragon?" hissed Beauchamp.

"Get the horse out of the shafts," ordered Pendragon.

Beauchamp did so, and tethered the animal next to his own to the branch of a nearby sapling. The three men manhandled the hay wain around until the front of it was tight against the wall, and the shafts were lying back over the vehicle with their blunt ends towards the tail board.

Prince Albert eyed the cart. "Not an easy jump. It will be essential to be accurate with the first step, to avoid the shafts."

"You'll never make it," said Beauchamp sadly. "I'll lay ten guineas to one the horses won't take the wall. And five to one says you'll go over without your mounts."

There was a soft chuckle from the Prince. "If you don't mind, Captain, I'll take your friend's second bet. If only to prove I'm an optimist."

Beauchamp unlashed the lances from beneath Prince Albert's saddle, and when the two men had remounted passed the weapons up to them. He handed them each one of the heavy sabres in their scabbards. The men belted them on. The pistols were already in the saddle holsters.

Beauchamp's normal enthusiasm had returned. "I say, 'Dragon, couldn't I climb the wall and fight on foot beside you?" he suggested.

Pendragon shook his head. "We'll need someone over here to keep watch," he said. "And if by any chance we shouldn't return, then someone to make a report."

"Damn," swore Beauchamp. "Well, anyway, happy hunting."

Pendragon walked his horse near to the tail of the hay wain, pausing briefly so that the animal might have an opportunity to gauge the height, and then trotted it back a full seventy yards from the wall. Prince Albert followed him. "Are you ready, Sir?" asked Pendragon.

The Prince grunted.

"Keep your lance point up as you jump. Let's go."

Pendragon pulled his horse's head round, kneed it to a canter, and as it lurched forward at gathering speed in the moonlight dug in his spurs, raking them along the animal's flank. It surged powerfully beneath him.

* * *

There was little time for thought now. Pendragon lifted his lance until it was well above the level of his animal's head. He used his spurs again, forcing the horse to its absolute maximum speed. The hay wain loomed ahead. He felt the animal hesitate, judge its distance and bunch its muscles; it launched itself upwards.

Its hooves hit the woodwork. The horse found itself suddenly confronted by yet another obstacle. It leapt again, desperately. The wall and spikes were beneath in the darkness, then it was falling. Pendragon leant backward as the horse dropped at a perilous angle. It hit the ground heavily, its forelegs buckling with its weight. It stumbled and Pendragon pulled at the reins. The animal recovered itself with a heave that almost unseated its rider. Pendragon swerved sideways, gripping so tightly with his knees that he felt skin being torn from his legs.

There was the thud of hooves on the hay wain behind him, then a whinny of fear from the Prince's horse. The sound was almost immediately followed by a heavy crash, and a curse in German. Pendragon jerked his horse around and kneed it back towards the wall. There was a dark heap close against the brick-work. The heap moved. Prince Albert staggered to his feet. His horse remained motionless.

Pendragon leapt from his animal and grabbed at Prince

140

Albert. The man shook him away fiercely. "Get on my horse," ordered Pendragon. There was no time for argument. He pushed at the Prince, forcing him to accept. He glanced at the other animal. It lay awkwardly with its head beneath its body. The neck was obviously broken. Pendragon handed the Prince his lance and drew his sabre. "A stirrup charge," he said. "Keep the speed regular. If I drop then don't hesitate, but keep on going until you reach the house. It will be straight ahead." He wedged his hand and forearm through the loop of the right hand stirrup, winding his wrist a couple of turns through the leather. He remembered briefly the stirrup charges he had seen in the Crimea. He had always thought them a frightening experience for the soldiers taking part. "Ready," he gasped, gripping the sabre hilt as tightly as he could.

Prince Albert dug his spurs into the horse. It jerked forward at a trot. Pendragon found himself covering the ground far faster than he could have run without the support of the stirrup.

"To the right," warned the Prince urgently. Pendragon could see a dark shape bound in ahead of them. "Leopard!"

He tried to judge the point where the charging leopard would meet them. He brought the sabre up and turned the blade sideways, aiming it at the animal. Now the horse was at a canter, Pendragon's strides were becoming longer and longer. Just as he aimed his sabre point, the Prince's lance point dropped in front of him. There was a feline shriek of agony from the leopard as the lance caught it a little below the chin, skewering through its chest to dig into the ground somewhere beneath it. The lance bowed, and snapped. Prince Albert tossed it away and Pendragon heard the rattle of metal as the man drew his sabre.

The Prince swung his sword to his left, at an animal out of Pendragon's sight and on the other side of the horse, then cursed as he missed his blow. The horse snorted with fear and increased its speed. There was a snarl beside Pendragon and he glanced down to find the second leopard running almost parallel with his legs, and only inches away. He could see the flash of its white teeth as its lips drew back and it changed direction to bound in for the attack.

Pendragon swung the sabre but the leopard darted away out of range, and turned immediately for another attack. It shone like black lamp oil in the moonlight, muscles rippling powerfully as it moved. It was at his side again. He hacked the sabre downwards, feeling the keen edge bite into bone as the heavy blade took the leopard across its head. The animal collapsed and was behind instantly.

Pendragon was covering the ground now in fifteen-foot paces. His left arm, wound through the stirrup leather, was being pulled from its socket. He looked upwards; the house was ahead. The wide steps leading up to the wrecked front door, were pale slabs. The ground was clear as they crossed the overgrown lawn. Prince Albert leant back and reined in the horse. Pendragon gratefully wrenched his arm free of the stirrup. He was breathless with the exertion of the charge. His legs felt as though they would buckle if he moved another step. He forced himself onwards at a run. The Prince followed, now on foot and leading his horse by the reins.

There was a movement ahead of them. A leopard which had been resting in the shadows of the doorway moved into the moonlight and faced them. For a second it appeared surprised, then bunched itself, leaping in a high arc towards Pendragon. Pendragon dropped to his knees on the steps, holding his sabre ahead of him. The charging leopard, its forepaws spread wide, filled the air in front of him. The sabre seemed to drive back, the hilt twisting in his hands and smashing so hard against his breastbone all the air was knocked from his lungs. The animal hit him; all teeth, claws and noise. He was flung backwards against the wall beside the steps. The stench of animal smothered him. He struggled wildly, trying to kick himself away from the snarling, spitting animal. Pain raked at his side as the leopard tore at him with its back legs. Its powerful front paws held him in a wrestler's grip around his shoulders. Its weight bent him backwards over the low wall, threatening to break his spine. The animal's head was against his own, its breath hot and stinking, and he felt teeth brush his cheek. The animal slumped suddenly, then dropped jerking and kicking to the ground; the kicking was uncoordinated. The leopard writhed and then lay still. Prince Albert stood above it, his sabre dark-bladed with blood. He reached out a hand and pulled Pendragon upright.

Pendragon was surprised to find his own blade through the leopard's body, between its ribs and foreleg. In the moonlight he could see the animal's head almost severed from its body where the Prince had struck it. He wondered briefly how close the man's sword had been to his own neck as the leopard died.

There was one more animal, thought Pendragon. One more in the darkness somewhere. He stepped into the doorway, paused and listened. There was no sound. Prince Albert was close beside him.

Pendragon moved cautiously across the rubble on the broken floorboards. He reached the hidden door leading through to Helm's great hall, and paused again. He lifted the catch and opened the door a few inches. The room was lit only by a single candle in a brass candlestick in the centre of the huge table. Draught from the open door snatched at the flame. He stepped inside. As he did so, there was a movement in the shadows at the far end of the room. A bulky figure who had been slumped down in one of the chairs jerked upwards.

"Mister Helm?" Cragg's voice, thick with sleep, grated the question.

Pendragon moved into the candlelight.

Cragg was startled by his unexpected appearance. "You?" There was a brief pause. "Where's Gaunt? Gaunt, are you here? What . . ." Cragg, now fully awake, made up his mind quickly. Pendragon was here unaccompanied, and uninvited. "So you come back, eh, Captain Pendragon? A little bit of your heroics, eh? Very foolish, and very foolish for your gentleman friend in the doorway, 'cos there's no doubt but you won't be away from here." Cragg pushed himself up from the chair and faced Pendragon.

Suddenly realising Cragg's intentions, Pendragon twisted sideways and rammed his shoulder against Prince Albert. The Prince staggered. As he did so, the front of Cragg's chest seemed to erupt in a burst of fire and smoke. Heavy bullets whistled past the two men and shattered the woodwork behind. Cragg swore loudly as he realised he had missed his opportunity.

"Not lucky, Cragg," said Pendragon. "You forgot a basic rule of war, never describe your special weapons to your enemy. Now put up your hands."

Cragg moved quickly for a man of his size. He turned and snatched at one of the weapons displayed on the wall beyond the table. There was the clatter of metal as a breastplate dropped and crashed to the floor. Cragg faced Pendragon holding an antique two-handed executioner's sword. He moved slowly forward, swinging the end of the broad weapon in a menacing arc.

The pistol? Pendragon damned himself for leaving the weapon in its holster on the horse's saddle. His brief fight with the leopard on the steps had removed all thought of it from his mind. "Don't try to get behind him," he shouted to the Prince. "He has a second pistol strapped on his back."

Cragg chuckled and leapt forward, the sword slicing the air a few inches from Pendragon's chest. From his right, Prince Albert struck at the heavy blade, but its weight brushed the cavalry sabre aside as though it were a feather. Using his great strength, Cragg stopped the swing of his sword and brought it upwards so fast Pendragon was forced to leap backwards to avoid being split apart. Cragg slowed the swing of the sword above his head. As he did so Pendragon hurled his sabre, underhand, letting go his hold on its hilt, and praying the weapon

144

would miss the thick leather pad supporting Cragg's chest pistol. Cragg stopped his movement, his huge sword poised above him. He looked surprised and took a step away from Pendragon. The sabre was buried halfway to its hilt in his chest. Cragg let his own sword drop and put his hands on the hilt of Pendragon's sabre. He began, his eyes wide and a determined look on his face, to pull the weapon from his chest. Just as it seemed he would succeed, his grip on the hilt relaxed. His mouth opened, gushing bright blood; his knees buckled and he fell sideways against the oak table. He slumped to the floor. There was a dreadful gurgling and he was motionless.

Pendragon snatched his sword from Cragg's body. There was a door on one side of the room and although he had never passed beyond it, he knew it could only lead to Helm's private apartments. He rammed it open. There was a narrow corridor lit by candles in an ironwork chandelier. There were three doors; two to the left, and one at the end of the passage. Pendragon opened them with caution. Behind each was a room, simply furnished; they were the living quarters of Helm's secret part of the seemingly derelict house.

He shook his head at Prince Albert. "All of them empty. There are two more rooms above." He ran through the long hall, and climbed the disguised staircase. As he had expected, Cragg's room was deserted. Pendragon tried the final one where he and Cox had been imprisoned. New external hinges had been fitted, to ensure that no future prisoners took the same action as had Pendragon and Cox. Pendragon slid aside the black iron bolt and pulled back the thick door. There was a sound in the darkness of the room.

"Who's in there?" Pendragon prayed it would be Georgina and Cox.

"Captain? Damn me, Sir. It's Cox, Captain." Cox appeared at the doorway, unshaven and grubby.

"And Miss Carr?" Prince Albert's question was urgent.

"Miss Carr? He took her with him, Captain. Helm and the others . . . they went off together, Sir. Left me with that bastard Cragg, as food for his animals. They said I wasn't no use to them." Cox sounded insulted.

"Where to, Cox? Have you any possible idea, man?" Pendragon demanded.

Cox hesitated. "Well yes, Sir. Cragg was laughing about it. Said the lady would find herself in an unaccustomed house, where Cragg thought all women should as likely be kept. He didn't exactly say, but I gathered it was the brothel you and I passed through from the Holy Land. He seemed to think it was a good joke, Captain, and made a few remarks that shouldn't be made about ladies such as Miss Carr."

"Brothel?" Prince Albert sounded horrified. "Miss Carr in a brothel, Captain? Is Helm also a white slaver?"

"I think not, Sir," replied Pendragon. "Though he may be when the chance presents itself. No, I think this time he is simply using the place as yet another hideaway. It is more central than here, and more suitable for a party their size. Perhaps he is being cautious and anticipating the possibility of such a rescue attempt."

Prince Albert refused to be appeased. "A brothel," he repeated, his voice hard. "Taking Georgina to a place like that is unforgivable." He spoke as though it was the final effrontery, more serious even than the attempt on his life. "And you know of the whereabouts of this, this place, Captain?"

"Yes, Sir."

"Then we must go there, and at once. I cannot tolerate this further insult to Miss Carr. She must be in the depths of despair."

"Are you still fit, Cox?" asked Pendragon.

"Me fit, Captain? Of course, Sir! Though I admit to a slight thirst as I've had no water for more than twenty-four hours."

"Then come on, Cox. We'll find something for you when we

146

get outside. All the leopards, bar one of the beasts, are dead. We must be prepared for the final animal, and then we will be free of this damned place."

"Cragg, Captain Sir?"

"Dead," answered Prince Albert. "By your master's hand, though I wish it had been my own."

* * *

The horse was still standing at the top of the steps of the house. It pranced nervously as they approached but calmed as soon as Prince Albert took it by the bit ring. Pendragon unbuckled the holster on the saddle and drew out the heavy cavalry pistol. He passed his sabre to Cox.

The three men walked back towards the wall. The moon was fully risen and the shadows beneath the trees compact and sharp edged. A few yards into the woods the horse skipped and jerked its head, trying to break away from them. The body of one of the leopards lay in the undergrowth, the grass smeared dark where it had kicked in its final agonies.

There was no sign of the remaining animal until they were within a few yards of the wall, when they heard a sharp and warning snarl.

" 'Dragon?" It was Beauchamp's voice from ahead of them.

"Yes," shouted Pendragon.

There was an explosion and a flash of flame. Below the wall something thrashed and struggled. Beauchamp shouted excitedly. "I got him, damned animal! I've been sitting here the last twenty minutes listening to him feeding on Fat Arse's hunter. Damn me, Pendragon, I didn't dare try a shot until I knew you were safe. Blast me, though, how do I explain away Fat Arse's hunter? Jove, that's a pretty rotten thing, 'Dragon; sorry, Colonel, your horse got eaten . . . he'll have me dashed hide as a trophy!"

Pendragon looked for the gates. He found them some fifty

yards along the wall. He blew the first lock off with a pistol shot, reloaded the weapon, and shattered the second mechanism.

Outside, Beauchamp was waiting on his horse. "Your aunt, 'Dragon, is she safe?"

Pendragon explained.

Beauchamp cursed their luck but then said, brightly, "At least, though, 'Dragon, there's still the two of us horsed, we can get to the dashed place pretty sharply and complete the mission."

There was a polite cough at Beauchamp's side, at about the level of his knee. Beauchamp looked down.

"If you don't mind, Lieutenant," said Prince Albert, politely. "I will be grateful if you will dismount. I am in need of a horse, though not exactly offering my kingdom."

"Of course," answered Beauchamp. He slid from the saddle and waited until Prince Albert was seated above him. "Well, 'Dragon? What do you say, old fellow? Shall we all go? I suppose I can ride that damned cottager's beast."

There was a clink of coins. "I believe I owe you a guinea, Sir." Prince Albert handed a single coin to the surprised Beauchamp. "And now if you'll excuse me . . ." He dug his knees into Beauchamp's horse and cantered it away.

"I say . . ." began Beauchamp. " 'Dragon, what the dashed hell?"

"Sorry, old lad. Here, swap coats with me, will you? I can't go visiting with it torn to shreds and bloodstained." Pendragon tossed Beauchamp his topcoat; it was little more than a rag.

"Oh, damn, 'Dragon! Damn and blast!" Beauchamp frowned, took off his own coat and handed it to Pendragon. "Oh, see here, 'Dragon . . ."

"It's got to be just the two of us," apologised Pendragon. "I wish you could come along, but you'll never keep up on that farm nag. Must hurry, the fellow doesn't know the way! Take care of Lieutenant Beauchamp, Cox, will you; take him home and give him a brandy or two." Pendragon swung himself on to his horse and shook the reins.

"Here . . . I say, 'Dragon!" began Beauchamp. He threw Pendragon's coat on to the ground angrily. "Oh, what the hell . . ."

Cox interrupted him. "Shouldn't waste your breath, Sir. You know the Captain once he has the bit between his teeth, and the other gentleman seems the same." He stopped and picked up Pendragon's coat. "Here, Sir. You'll need this. It'll be chilly by the time we get back. We'll be lucky to make London in two hours with the pair of us on that horse."

"Oh, damn me!" groaned Beauchamp. He swung Pendragon's coat around his shoulders like a tattered cloak.

7

THE MOON, AUTUMN GOLD, seemed larger now as it dropped towards the horizon beyond the first of London's buildings. It was one-thirty in the morning, with dawn only a few hours ahead. There was no doubt as to Prince Albert's anxiety for he kept his horse moving at an awkward pace, a little too fast for a trot, and yet below a full canter. It was the sort of speed known to cavalrymen as an animal killer, for even the best mount was incapable of keeping it up for great distances without regular rest periods.

Pendragon's knees, skinned first a few days ago on his ride from Hampshire, and again as he gripped his saddle on the jump over the wall, were raw and bleeding. The discomfort painfully reminded him of his early days of cavalry training when such skinning was accepted as normal until the rider's knees developed thick callouses.

The city was visible again now. Towards the east the sky was hazy below the moon with the smoke of the continual factory fires kept stoked and working throughout the night. A glow from distant furnaces beyond Rotherhythe provided a rosy aura. Already the sulphurous smell of the city mingled with the scent of the fields.

Pendragon was more nervous of Prince Albert's presence now.

It had been bad enough before and a deadly risk to the Prince's life, but somehow, away from the city, the dangers had not seemed so pronounced, so concentrated. There was no possibility of changing the man's mind; he refused stubbornly to withdraw and leave the remainder of the problem to Pendragon. Had the threats to the Prince's life not been so serious Pendragon would have found his attitude intriguing. The man was no longer a Prince but an adventurer, and although an unlikely companion on such an escapade, Pendragon realised that even had he made his own choice there were few men he could have found as able and daring. In many ways it was a great pity the man's actions would be concealed from the public; they would have ensured his popularity beside their Queen, and killed for ever the view that he was stiff and arrogant.

Though still four hours from daylight, London was awake; if it ever, in fact, really slept. Passing a narrow alley off the Marylebone Road, the two riders could see a group of costers, working by gas flares, loading their barrows with vegetables for the day's work ahead of them. Their women and children worked beside them, their shouted orders and conversation showing that they cared little for any of the neighbours who might still be in their beds.

At Park Crescent Pendragon turned right into Portland Place. Here the big houses of the wealthy were in darkness; it would be three hours more before kitchen maids began their labours in the basements, and housemaids their cleaning and tidying in the grand rooms of the residences.

It was almost two-thirty by the time the men reached Oxford Street. A slight mist had formed, giving silver halos to the gas lights and swirling around the horses' legs as they moved. The sound of their hoofbeats echoed from the buildings.

For the first few miles of the journey Prince Albert had ridden ahead, forcing Pendragon to encourage his horse to keep up with the man. Now they were in London itself, and the Prince was uncertain of the whereabouts of the brothel, he rode beside Pendragon, becoming angry if Pendragon allowed his animal to slacken its pace.

It was not difficult for Pendragon to find the brothel, although in construction and size it was identical to every other building for a hundred yards on either side. It was as well lit as any gin palace; the row of carriages outside, waiting the night away while their masters caroused, designated the hostel's trade. It was a tall building, six storeys high from the basement level, built of red brick. Most of the windows, although curtained, showed lights. The main entrance itself was lit by two ornate and gilded lamps. The only darkness came from the basement area, behind a row of cast-iron railings, where steps led down to the tradesmen's entrance and the kitchens.

Pendragon stopped his horse beside the last of the waiting carriages. The coachman was asleep, leaning sideways in his seat and snoring loudly. Pendragon reached out and shook the man gently.

"Right, Sir! Home it is, Sir. Hope you had . . ."

"I'm not your master," said Pendragon. The man peered at him curiously. "Will you watch our horses for us? For a payment!"

"Yes, Sirs," replied the man, sleepily. "Though I can only stay as long as my master allows. If you ties them to the railings they'll be fine, I'd say." The man, now awake, eyed Pendragon strangely. "Beg your pardon, Sir, but if you're thinking of going inside, I know they won't take kindly to your cutlasses."

Pendragon passed the man his shilling, dismounted and unstrapped his sabre, pushing it through the saddle girth. He indicated to the Prince to do likewise, but tapped the pistol holster to indicate that they should not enter unarmed. The Prince nodded and thrust one of the weapons out of sight in his waistband. Pendragon, who had reloaded Beauchamp's pistol as he rode, did likewise.

The coachman who had watched them dismount was dozing again. Pendragon moved quickly, pushing open the low iron gate leading down to the basement. He slipped through and jumped the steps to the shadows below. Prince Albert followed him.

"It's a large place. Where do we begin looking?" The Prince whispered his question.

"Search as we go," answered Pendragon. "It's all we can do." He tried the door catch. It turned, but the door was bolted on the inside. "Pray, Sir," hissed Pendragon. He leant his arm hard against a pane of glass to deaden the noise, then hit the edge of the glass with his knuckles. The glass broke with a dull crack, but the linseed oil putty prevented fragments of the glass from dropping inside the door. Pendragon paused for a few seconds, listening, and eased a fragment of the glass inwards until it broke free and he was able to lift it out silently. He removed more until he could get his arm through the window. "A trick I learnt in Paris, Sir," he whispered. "You hit the glass near the edge, not the centre. A knack of French burglars, Sir." There was a grating noise as he slid back a bolt, and then the door was open.

Pendragon moved inside cautiously. The place was pitch dark and he would have been glad of a lantern. He stepped towards a door on the far side of the room. A slim bar of light showed beneath the woodwork. He was reaching for the door handle when a shadow moved in the light below the door, and the door was pushed open suddenly from the far side. A figure carrying a lighted candle in a holder stepped into the room at Pendragon's side. There was no time for hesitation; he struck hard with his pistol butt and felt it crunch against the figure's skull. He caught the body as it crumpled, but was unable to prevent the clatter of the candle holder dropping to the stone floor. He paused, listening, but there was no other sound nearby, only a ripple of laughter on some higher floor.

He dragged the body away from the doorway, feeling relief

as he discovered it was a man. For a flash of a second as he struck he had realised it could easily be a kitchen maid, but the urgency of the situation gave him no choice. Discovery by a woman, or man, would be just as dangerous at this stage of the game. He wondered whether his blow had been too vicious, but with his fingertips he could still feel the strong pumping of blood in a vein in the man's neck.

He re-lit the candle, keeping the light low on the floor, and searched for suitable materials to bind the man; to have him regain consciousness and raise the alarm would be disastrous. A narrow strip of kitchen towelling hanging near a sink served as rope. Pendragon gagged the man with a wadding of floor cloth and rolled him under the scullery table.

Once clear of the kitchens, Pendragon knew discovery was less likely to cause alarm. Unless the Prince himself was recognised they might be normal clients, a little drunk perhaps and untidy as a result of horseplay. They could always claim to have lost their way within the buildings. It would be something which must happen frequently. Few of the brothel's clients were completely sober, and most would be drunk almost to the point where their expense on a woman would be a waste of money.

He stopped in the doorway and brushed some of the dust from his clothing. Prince Albert did likewise. With luck, now, they would pass as a couple of wealthy 'bloods' on a night's escapading.

Pendragon recognised the narrow hall as the part of the building where he had first entered, emerging from the flap above the secret cellar. It was covered by the same length of carpet Cragg kicked into place, but he could see a faint outline of the cellar flap through the thin pile of the gaudy material.

Ahead was the flight of stairs leading to the main hallway of the brothel. He straightened his shoulders, put his hands behind his back, and tried to look as casual as possible. On the floor above he knew there was the large reception lounge and nothing else. The bedrooms, and any private rooms which Helm might use, would be on higher floors; he guessed Helm would choose the top floor where he was less likely to be bothered by the comings and goings of the brothel's clients.

Pendragon and the Prince reached the head of the serving stairs. The hallway was empty, although the murmur of conversation came from behind the double doors of the lounge. The staircase leading to the higher floors faced the entrance to the room, and the two men, now side by side, strolled towards it.

They were within a foot of reaching the staircase when a young woman, her hair dyed a bright and impossible scarlet, appeared at the lounge door. Her eyes, ringed by make-up above thickly rouged cheeks, widened in simulated pleasure. She ran a moist tongue over her lips to give them a shine.

"Here . . . hello." She eyed the two men, smiling, then winked grotesquely. She walked forward quickly and pushed herself between them, slipping her arms through theirs. "Well, well, now. And how did I miss you two handsome beauties? Are you for gaming, my pretty gentlemen, or are you for games?" She raised her voice and called through the lounge doors. "Dorrie! Hey there, Dorrie . . . come and see what I've found for us."

A second girl, far younger than the first and probably only fifteen or sixteen years old, pushed a white face around the edge of one of the doors.

"Well then," said the first woman, loudly. "Don't hang about. Come and meet my gentlemen. This is Dorrie, Sir," she said to Pendragon. "You'll like her, she's cheeky—all over!" she winked at him again, released his arm and firmly anchored herself to Prince Albert.

"Madam." Pendragon nodded to the younger girl.

"There, what did I say," said the first woman, happily. "Gentlemen, as like as not, the pair of them." She looked up at Prince Albert. "Would you be a gentleman, darling?"

"I believe so, Ma'am," replied the Prince, coolly.

155

"Good, then, darlings." The woman peered into Prince Albert's face. "I'm Charlotte. What a bloody name for a girl in my profession! Don't half get some funny remarks! I used to call myself Lottie, but no one was fooled, so it was back to Charlotte. This is Dorrie. She's my cousin. Have you two gentlemen just arrived?" She looked at Pendragon strangely. "I never saw you both come in."

"We arrived a little while ago, and were having a look around," replied Pendragon, making his voice as friendly and warm as possible. "Isn't that right?" he said brightly to Prince Albert, hoping his tone of voice would give the man some sort of a lead. So far, the Prince was behaving so coldly towards the women that he was quite likely to arouse suspicion.

"Er, yes, quite . . ." replied the Prince, making an obvious effort.

" 'Ere, is he your Dad, then?" asked the girl Dorrie.

Prince Albert laughed and the older woman giggled.

"A friend," said Pendragon.

"D'you want to game, then?" asked Charlotte. "Or were you thinking of a little slap and tickle? Either's all right with both of us, 'less of course you don't fancy us, which would be a pity, really. Here . . ." she looked closely at Prince Albert and for a terrifying second Pendragon thought she had recognised him. "You ain't half a fierce looking cove! You ain't an undertaker, are you? I don't like undertakers, personally."

Dorrie had stationed herself on Pendragon's arm. She spoke confidentially. "Charlotte don't go with undertakers. She's superstitious."

"We're both military," said Pendragon.

"H'officers? Oh, how lovely. We like officers, don't we, Dorrie? Goin' to keep your spurs on?" She shrieked with laughter. "Oo, my poor bum! "

"I think we must try your gaming room," suggested Pendragon. The longer they remained in the hall, the more likely

156

they would be noticed. At least a move to the gaming room would give them time to think of a way to lose the two women.

"Good," shrilled Charlotte. She shook her red hair around her shoulders and flicked at it with her free hand. "You accompany the young gentleman, Dorrie. I shall remain with this fierce h'officer, who is probably very high ranking. My goodness, but just look at him, and see his fierceness." She giggled again. "We shall have to test you, won't we, darling, later?" Holding the Prince firmly by his arm, she steered him up the stairs. He walked stiffly erect, his head up and his shoulders exactly square, as though the staircase led to an executioner's block. Pendragon could not suppress a smile.

*   *   *

The gaming room seemed to occupy the entire floor above the reception lounge, with the stairs entering it at one side. No doubt at some previous time there had been a hallway or landing, but to make use of additional space any dividing walls which might have existed had been removed.

Pendragon, conscious that Beauchamp's coat was anything but a good fit, was pleased to see that apart from the ornately shaded gas lamps above the tables and playing areas it was far more dimly illuminated than the lounge; perhaps with the incongruous thought that clients might prefer anonymity while they lost their money, whereas the greater light below was necessary for their selection of a night's companion. Pendragon was able to relax a little, for unless a player leant forward over the table his face was in the shadows cast by the brass shades.

For such a late hour of the night—or early hour of the morning—the room was surprisingly busy. In one distant corner a large group of card players leant sleepily back in their chairs, moving only occasionally to toss their cards on to the green baize, or to reach out to slide bets across the table. The centre of the room was dominated by a gaudily decorated numbers wheel, spinning and clicking as a girl drummed her fingers against the revolving disc. Several men, with female companions, stood noisily encouraging one of their friends to lay heavy bets against the house. Dice rattled on tables beside the staircase. The air was heavy with the smell of cigar smoke and a conglomeration of fifty varieties of perfumes.

"Well, gentlemen, what's it to be?" asked Charlotte, waving her arms expansively. "Take your choice, darlings. Dice, cards, the wheel? Name your game for me, and it'll be played, bless your eyes. There's a rat and terrier pit in a back room, and a couple of guineas will buy you three dozen fresh caught squeakers. There's a choice of six young dogs, though personally I'd not guarantee them too lively at this late hour. Can't offer you cock-fighting, though it could be arranged for another time."

"Perhaps the numbers, for a little while anyway." Pendragon glanced at Prince Albert and shrugged slightly. The Prince nodded, almost imperceptibly. There was no present way of escaping the company of the two women.

The small crowd of men and women moved to one side for them as they approached the wheel. The instrument stopped, and the single gambler swore at his companions' laughter at his misfortune. The girl operating the wheel tried persuading him to bet yet again, but the man shook his head and indicated he would wait to see the luck of the newcomers.

There was a low coloured table in front of the wheel, divided into squares and numbers matching those on the wheel itself. Pendragon felt in his pocket for change and was a little annoyed to find he had only guineas in his pockets, and no silver coins. He slid a guinea on to one of the numbers. Prince Albert shook his head. The girl at the wheel smiled and started it spinning. It clicked noisily, to stop on Pendragon's choice.

There was a murmur from the watchers. The girl slid a pile of counters towards Pendragon. Damn! It was far more convenient, and certainly safer, to lose at this moment. "Leave them on the number, please," he said. The girl nodded.

Dorrie jogged at Pendragon's arm, excitedly. "Here, you just won twenty-five gold 'uns. Like as not you're throwing 'em back. Use them to buy me a present."

The wheel spun again. Pendragon smiled grimly.

The wheel stopped on the same number. The operator stared at it, surprised. The small audience murmured. Pendragon looked at Prince Albert, but the man's face was expressionless and gave no indications of his feelings.

"My God," said Dorrie. "Look what you've gone and done."

Charlotte let go her hold on Prince Albert's arm and grabbed at Pendragon. "You know what you've got, darlin'?" She dabbed at her fingertips, counting rapidly. "That's six hundred and fifty guineas including your own coin. Take it off, take it off, now."

The operator was sliding black counters across to him. Each marked with a gold twenty-five. Pendragon clenched his fists. At any normal time he would have been delighted but now it was an embarrassment.

"They're all on, still," he said. "The same number." It was unlikely to come up a third time.

"You're mad, ducks, plain mad," said Dorrie looking wildly around. "He's cold stone raving."

The number came up for the third time!

There was so much commotion players from the other tables joined those around the wheel.

The girl at the wheel had a look of incredulity on her face.

"Sixteen thousand, two hundred and fifty guineas, Sir."

There was a movement beside her and a short man, perhaps foreign, wearing the red sash indicating he was one of the house croupiers, joined the girl. He spoke to her for a moment and turned to Pendragon.

"Your winnings are sixteen thousand two hundred and fifty guineas Sir. It's above the amount we are allowed to accept on a single number. You can bet a colour at even money, Sir, or drop your bet down to ten guineas."

Blast the wheel, thought Pendragon. This was just the attention he had wished to avoid! He decided quickly. It was easier and safer to let the money ride yet again, this time on a colour, and hope he would lose. The amount, marvellous as it would be in normal circumstances, was of no importance now. "It's all on red," he told the man.

The man barely acknowledged the bet, reaching behind him and spinning the wheel so rapidly the numbers were a band of black on its circumference. The audience was completely silent as the wheel began to slow down. For a second, Pendragon wondered if the wheel was spiked and his loss perhaps guaranteed by the man's action. He hoped it was so.

The wheel slowed until the colours and numbers could be clearly seen. It trickled past a black, moving almost imperceptibly, and stopped with the silver pointer directly over a red.

The man bit his lip. The crowd roared their approval. The man bowed. "You have won, Sir. Thirty-two thousand, five hundred guineas. I'm afraid we must close the wheel for tonight, Sir. If you should care to try it tomorrow, it will be open again, Sir. Perhaps you would like to play another game? Cards, perhaps?"

"Thirty-two thousand five hundred guineas," whispered Dorrie. She hung on Pendragon's arm as though she were fainting. She looked up at his face. " 'Ere, darlin', will we be celebrating with champagne?"

The crowd was pressing around Pendragon, calling out their congratulations. Prince Albert hissed in his ear. "What now, Captain?"

"Let's get away from here," whispered Pendragon to Dorrie.

"The crowd's too much." He faced the croupier. "I shall collect my winnings later on." The man nodded.

Dorrie pulled at Pendragon's arm. "Upstairs, darling? We can have a room there, and champagne sent up to us. That'd be nice." She giggled again. "Will I get a little of the winnings, for being your lucky charm? A few new dresses?"

Pendragon pushed his way through the crowd. It seemed as though everyone in the room was trying to touch him to better their own luck. The women watched Charlotte and Dorrie enviously. Dorrie, enjoying the sensation, was cool towards them, tossing her hair arrogantly as she passed.

They climbed a further two flights of stairs before Charlotte stopped them in front of one of the doors. She turned to Dorrie. "Off you go with him then," she said jerking her head at Prince Albert.

Dorrie stiffened angrily. " 'Ere, what you on about? This gentleman's with me. He's been with me right along."

Charlotte took hold of Pendragon's other arm firmly. "Nonsense," she snapped. "I met *this* gentleman at the door. I called you, remember?"

"Why, you . . ." began Dorrie, swinging back her arm.

"Enough." Pendragon stepped between the two women who were glaring at each other like alley cats before a fight. "We'll all stay together. The four of us. Is this the room?" Before they could answer him, he had removed both their arms from his own, opened the door and ushered them inside.

The room was lushly furnished. It was neither drawing room or bedroom but a combination of both, with armchairs, sofa and a huge bed. The ceiling was high and ornately plastered in poor taste with painted fat cherubs gorging at some strange eastern feast. The wall-covering was of Chinese silk. A fire burned brightly in the grate.

"Nice, isn't it?" said Dorrie to Pendragon. "Really for two," she said pointedly, glaring at Charlotte.

Pendragon closed the door behind them.

"Champagne, then. Shall I ring and order some?" Before he could reply, Charlotte had jerked at a narrow silk rope. "There, that'll be better. How many bottles. Two? Four?"

"Six," said Dorrie. "Because six is my lucky number ... and four isn't yours, ducky." She looked threateningly at Charlotte.

"No arguments, either of you," Pendragon warned.

"A cigar for the gentlemen," shrilled Dorrie. She opened one of the drawers of a roll-top desk and found a box. She waved a cigar at Pendragon. "You're almost a millionaire, darling. How about that? Almost a millionaire. Me? I never earned more than a hundred pounds a year in my life. Over thirty-two thousand pounds ..." she said it as though she were dreaming. "Just think about that. A house and a carriage ... an' real skivvies!"

There was a discreet tap at the door. Charlotte answered it hurriedly. "Yes, champagne," she said to some unseen brothel servant outside. "Six bottles of the very best. Pink, I'd say." She looked back over her shoulder at Pendragon. "Pink?"

"Pink," he replied wearily.

Charlotte swirled off her silk shawl. "Let's play a game or something. Shall I think of a game, darlings? A game four can play." She hummed to herself for a second. "A charade." She pirouetted, then reached and quickly unbuttoned the back of her dress. "Help me then, darling. I want to be a statue. Greek," she said seductively to Prince Albert. "And quite naturally undressed." She pulled at her dress so roughly Pendragon could hear the material tearing.

Dorrie turned to Pendragon. "And you shall undress me, for we shall both be Greek statues. And you will see how lucky you really are."

"Well," said Charlotte, "we have to begin somewhere, don't we? Statues are as good as anything else for starters."

"Just one minute, ladies, please." The girls were already naked to the waist and had to be stopped now, before everything

162

got completely out of hand. "I was the winner, and I think I should be the one to choose the games." Pendragon spoke firmly.

Prince Albert's face was bright pink as though he was holding his breath and about to explode with the effort.

The girls paused in their stripping, each of them standing in a small pile of clothing, as though their proposed game of statues had already started.

"Well?" asked Dorrie. "All right, darling, you choose." She stood upright and put her hands on her hips. Her body was as white as her face, her breasts pert and small nippled. The effect was spoilt by bruising on her ribs which could only have been caused by rough fingers.

"I was, er, thinking," Pendragon said. He risked a brief glance at the Prince and wondered what in fact *he* was thinking. "I suggest a military kind of game, seeing that we are both military men."

"A military game, oh good," shrieked Charlotte. She was plumper and bigger breasted than Dorrie. Her body seemed to have more colour and warmth. "What is a military game?"

"We would have to tie you both up." Pendragon smiled at them wickedly.

"Tie us up . . ." Charlotte grimaced.

"Quite gently, of course," added Pendragon, winking at her. "We wouldn't be at all rough."

"I wouldn't mind if you were," giggled Dorrie, thinking of his enormous winnings. "You can be rough, if you're not really too cruel."

"Do you want to beat us?" asked Charlotte curiously. Dorrie's enthusiasm warned her that to hesitate might be to lose Pendragon to the younger girl. She became determined not to be outdone. She laughed. "Well, darling, I don't mind either. In fact, a beating can be good for a girl . . . encourages her, I like to think." She turned suddenly, bent over and tossed her skirts and

163

petticoats over her head. White bloomers stretched tight across her thighs. She twisted upright again and grinned at Pendragon. "Like that, darling? Over the end of the bed, or across your knee? Dressed as I am so you can pull them down yourself, or naked as the day I was born? Like I said, absolutely anything will be all right by me."

Pendragon felt himself blush. "Er, as I suggested; tied, I think."

"Then tied it shall be," squeaked Dorrie, competing with Charlotte for his attention. "Hurrah!" She ran across the room to the windows and pulled off the gold cords used to tie the curtains back in daytime. She tossed them to Pendragon. "Tie me first, darling. On the bed. And tie me face downwards, with my arms and legs spread to the corners." She pushed her remaining clothing down and off in one movement taking Pendragon completely by surprise. She faced him for a second, completely naked. "Like this!" She ran to the bed, laughing, and threw herself down upon it, bouncing wildly on the mattress. She reached out her hands to grasp the brass rails. "You'll have to feed me the champagne when it comes."

Pendragon shrugged weakly at Prince Albert, who was watching the scene in obvious horror.

Charlotte was searching for material for her own bonds. She dragged a chair over to the wall, climbed on it and unhooked the bell pull, returning to hand it to Pendragon. "Tie her first," she said softly.

Pendragon walked to the bed and tied the willing Dorrie to the rails. He pulled the cords tight around her wrists and ankles, but she giggled joyfully, twisting her body on the linen covers, until her buttocks quivered with her efforts.

Charlotte's voice hardened slightly. "Let me cork the bottle for you." She reached down to the floor and snatched up a kerchief which had been in her bodice. She walked to the bed, glared down for a second at Dorrie, and forced the kerchief

164

roughly into the struggling girl's mouth. She stopped and ripped a piece of cloth from the hem on one of Dorrie's discarded petticoats, and tied it firmly over the kerchief, around the girl's head. She smiled sweetly at Pendragon. "Wouldn't you enjoy it far better if I were to beat her first?" She spoke with enthusiasm. "And, if you thought I was being too kind, then you could beat her yourselves afterwards." She bent down over the silent but wide-eyed Dorrie. "You little cow," she said. She looked at Pendragon, almost pleading with him to agree to her request.

"I . . ." began Pendragon, nervously.

Prince Albert interrupted, speaking for the first time since they had entered the room. "Young lady, you forget who are the masters here. The pleasure of the beating is ours. I must remind you to conduct yourself correctly. Now please lay yourself over the end of the bed."

"You sure he ain't no undertaker?" asked Charlotte. She sighed, then shrugged and turned to face the end of the bed. She swung her skirts and petticoats up again and bent forward over the brass rails.

"Thank you," said the Prince, without emotion. He took the bell pull cord and tied the woman's hands to the inside of the foot rail, then he led the cord downwards and secured her ankles.

"You're really very strong," said Charlotte in a husky and subdued voice. "I hope, darlings, you don't intend to go too far. I mean, well, be as rough as you like, in a gentle sort of way. And, Lord above, I'm a lady, not a cavalry horse; I was only jokin' about them spurs! "

"Of course you were, Madam," replied the Prince, pleasantly. He took his kerchief from his breast pocket. "Quite clean and hygienic, Madam." As she opened her mouth to protest, he wedged it neatly inside. She shook her head violently and mumbled through the material. The Prince carefully ripped off another length of petticoat strip and tied the kerchief in place.

He brushed her skirts back into place over her rump, then turned to Pendragon and raised an eyebrow quizzically. "I trust, Captain, that this is all you intend?"

"Quite all, Sir," answered Pendragon with relief. "I couldn't think of any better way of getting them off our hands."

Prince Albert stared at the bed with its wriggling naked flesh. "I thank heavens sometimes my wife is unable to see quite into the minds of her officers." He paused and grinned at Pendragon. "And that of her husband, too," he added.

* * *

There was another sound beyond the door. Pendragon reached for his pistol and remembered the champagne. He cautiously opened the door a few inches. A serving trolley laden with bottles and glasses stood outside; there was no sign of the servant. He pulled the trolley into the room.

"I think we can begin our search, Sir," he said.

8

THERE WAS NO POSSIBLE chance of escape for the Prince or Pendragon. Four men faced them at the head of the staircase. The first of the men, the stocky croupier who had finally refused a further bet from Pendragon at the numbers wheel, made a forced effort to smile.

"Ah, the young gentleman with the luck. I was coming to call you, Sir. With wins as large as your own, it is normal for the accounting to be made by our Director himself. He has asked me to bring you to him. I'm glad we have not disturbed your pleasure in any way." The man was only a few feet from them now and, although the tone of his voice was superficially friendly, it barely concealed the fact that he would not be refused the invitation.

With the four men standing in their present position it might have been possible for Pendragon to rush them, in the hope at least a couple of them would be thrown backwards down the wide staircase, while the remainder could then be disposed of on equal terms by the Prince and himself. The odds were not impossibly against the manoeuvre, but Pendragon realised such action would certainly necessitate their immediate flight, and could in no way assist their search for Georgina. He bowed his head in acknowledgment. "We had just decided to leave," he said politely. "Your arrival is quite timely."

The man, unexpectedly, did not lead them down the stairs, but instead took them further along the corridor, back past the room in which the two women were still bound. There was no sound of their struggles, and Pendragon was certain the walls and doors of the rooms had been soundproofed. "I don't think you are a regular customer of ours, Sir," said the croupier. "I recognise most."

"Second visit. Last time I won nothing."

The croupier laughed. "But made up for it this time. If all our clients were as lucky, we'd be bankrupt in a few days. Yours is the largest winning we have had in several months. Let me see, the last of considerable size was . . ."

"Admiral Post-Howard," said one of the other men.

The croupier glared at him. "I'm sorry, Sir," he said to Pendragon, "I was about to state the amount, not the identity of the winner himself. Discretion, of course, Sir. Ah . . ." he paused outside a door. "Here we are, Sir."

Post-Howard! Pendragon remembered, the Admiral was dead; he had been killed in mysterious circumstances some months previously. It was obvious, too, that the name was familiar to Prince Albert for he opened his mouth as though to speak and then changed his mind.

There was no time for further speculation. The croupier pushed open a door. "The winning young gentleman, Sir, and his friend," he announced, stepping sideways so that Pendragon and Prince Albert could enter the room.

"Wait outside," a voice ordered the croupiers.

A man who had been sitting behind a heavy mahogany desk, stood and extended his hand towards Pendragon. He smiled the kind of smile Pendragon had seen on faces of market traders who had just lost a bargaining contest for the price of their goods.

"Good evening, Sirs . . . or better, good morning to you. My sincerest congratulations. A very large amount of money, but

168

have no fear, our croupiers will act as your guards on your way home. You will be safe from attack by any thieves or robbers. And now, Sir." The man brought Pendragon to the desk, still holding his hand, and putting his arm across Pendragon's shoulders as though they were old and familiar friends. It was an action which angered Pendragon, but as he reached the desk again the man released him and threw back the lid of a small oak box. He drew out several thick wads of banker's notes. "I trust these will be satisfactory, Sir. It is all in Bank of England one hundred pound notes. Please count them. I hear you placed your bet in gold; I trust, however, you do not want your winnings in like coin? It would take a barrow to carry them home. By the way, Sir, I do not believe you have given us your name. I would like it for our records."

"It is Pendragon, an ex-Captain of the 11th Hussars," said a voice from slightly behind them.

Pendragon turned. Two men had entered from a concealed door in the corner of the room. One was Selwyn, the man who had accompanied the German Count Von Oberstein; the other was James Helm.

*   *   *

The man at the desk spoke. "Ah, how opportune. I am about to pour glasses of brandy for these lucky gentlemen. The, er, Captain, did you say? He has won a great deal of money from us. A very large amount."

Helm faced Pendragon. His eyes were threatening. Pendragon stared back, giving the man no satisfaction. "So you have been gambling again, Captain," said Helm. "And now you can see you have lost once more."

"No," interrupted the Director. "He is a winner, my friend; thirty-two thousand, five hundred pounds. The gentleman I told you about a little while ago."

"Forgive me, but you are not in possession of the facts. I am correct when I say this man has lost. Captain Pendragon will himself agree. His friend too, has lost, whoever he is. We will not, I am sure you will be pleased to learn, be paying out the large sum of money. Will we, gentlemen?" He addressed the last question to Prince Albert and Pendragon.

"It strikes me, Helm, that this gambling hole has strange ways of paying its bigger winners," Pendragon said casually. "I have been told Admiral Post-Howard was a winner at this establishment. It would be most interesting, Helm, to discover if the night he played was also the night his body was found in Kensington Gore with its skull broken. I suspect it will be so. Once the police have this fact, I have no doubt this place will rapidly be closed. And this gentleman," he pointed at the Director, "will undoubtedly be able to answer many of their questions."

"How does he know this?" asked the Director, startled.

Helm smiled confidently. "The Captain has a way of finding out things. But how he has learnt of that matter can easily be solved when we have more time. Pendragon, as you are not accompanied by my colleague Mister Gaunt, I must assume you left your residence without his knowledge. Quite naughty, Captain Pendragon, and to involve one of your friends is quite unchivalrous. Will the gentleman be so loyal when he knows the price he is now certain to pay?"

Prince Albert had almost been ignored by Helm and his companions, but now he spoke. His voice was an ice cold threat. "If you care to look at me, Sir, you will be abe to judge the value of friendship for yourself." The Prince had been standing with his arms folded across his chest. He now straightened himself, drawing the heavy pistol from his waistband. He aimed it, unwavering, at Helm's head. "Pray test my loyalty, Helm!"

* * *

For a few seconds there was silence. Selwyn and the Director were motionless, waiting for some sign from Helm as to what they should do. Pendragon saw Selwyn rock forward, almost imperceptibly, on to the balls of his feet, so that he could leap into movement if this was Helm's order. Prince Albert had made a mistake with his move; Helm was now as aware of this as Pendragon. By producing the pistol, aiming it, and substituting his speech for action, the Prince had already lost the initiative. He should have drawn the gun, and killed Helm at once. Helm now believed he was facing a man inexperienced in killing, who might be reluctant to do so unless absolutely necessary.

Helm's face had tautened fractionally in anticipation of the pistol shot. Now it relaxed and the man's arrogance returned. "I observe, Captain Pendragon, that your friend is holding a cavalry pistol. It contains only one charge. I wish to know how he intends to kill not only the three of us, but also the various men throughout the building who will assuredly come at my bidding."

Pendragon had no choice of action. To hesitate now would result in one of Helm's men killing the Prince. Helm's words had made it quite clear what he wanted next; they were an invitation to Selwyn or the Director to attack the man who threatened him. Pendragon leapt backwards and jerked out his own pistol.

The Director jumped sideways, wrenching open one of the desk's drawers. He snatched inside and brought up a small revolver. Pendragon fired without any conscious aim. The lead ball hit the Director fractionally below the top fold of his cravat and smashed him back against the wall; blood splattered in a red mist behind him. He slid to the floor, the front of his shirt smoking where the smouldering oiled wad had set fire to the material.

Helm dived for the pistol lying beside the dead man. Pendragon leapt forward and kicked upwards, feeling his boot sink into Helm's stomach. There was another heavy explosion behind him and for a fraction of a second, he half expected to feel the burning pain of a penetrating bullet.

A figure crashed against him, he turned to defend himself against the attack, but saw Selwyn bending slightly forward, his face a sick green colour, and his hands pressed against his chest. Blood spurted from between his fingers, spraying in thin gushes on to Pendragon's legs. He pushed the man away. Selwyn collapsed to sit crosslegged for a moment then fell backwards.

Helm was on his knees, crawling towards the pistol. Prince Albert barged Pendragon to one side, grabbed Helm by his collar and dragged him to his feet, spinning him around and ramming him against the wall. Helm struggled, wildly. The Prince slapped him several times, open-handed across the face. With astonishing strength he picked him from his feet and flung him contemptuously across the table top. He stood over him. "Where is she? Where is Miss Carr?"

Helm, his mouth and nose bleeding, stared upwards. "You won't live five minutes more," he threatened.

The Prince pulled him to his feet. "I shall live long enough to kill you if you don't speak." He grabbed Helm by his hair and bent his head backwards. There was a silver paperknife resting on the desk's leather top. The Prince brought the keen point up under Helm's chin. "I do not share most Englishmen's hatred of the knife, Helm." He pressed the point into Helm's flesh until a trickle of blood ran down the man's throat. "You have ten seconds to speak; after that I shall drive the blade up through your chin and into the roof of your mouth. I warn you the pain will be quite terrible until the point reaches your brain."

Pendragon watched, startled by the Prince's viciousness. To interfere now, he realised, might be to silence Helm just as he might decide to speak.

"Five seconds," warned the Prince. He jammed the knife point deeper.

Helm squealed as the tip of the blade reached some hidden nerve. "Yes." His voice was high pitched with pain, and dis-

172

torted as he tried to tear his head free from Prince Albert's strong grasp. "Yes . . . yes."

The Prince pulled the knife away, but continued to hold Helm by the hair. "Where is she?" He twisted Helm's head backwards again.

"The basement," groaned Helm. "In a cellar."

"Damn," swore Pendragon. "We walked over the thing."

There was a hammering at the door and one of the centre panels was splintering. "Locked," explained the Prince. "I took the precaution while you and the Director were discussing your winnings. Didn't trust those men outside." He searched Helm's clothing for weapons, but found none.

Pendragon had the Director's small revolver in his hand. He now aimed it between Helm's eyes. "The way out, Helm? You lead, and the slightest hesitation will be your death!" The door was beginning to shatter near the lock. He pushed Helm around, and towards the hidden door where he and Selwyn had entered. Selwyn's body lay across the entrance. A stiletto, which Pendragon recognised as the one which Helm had pressed against Georgina's hand, had slipped from a pocket and lay in a pool of congealing blood.

Once inside the passage, Pendragon slammed the secret panel closed. He saw it had bolts, and slid them into place. He paused while Prince Albert hurriedly reloaded the two cavalry weapons, and then pushed his pistol against Helm's back. "Which way?"

"There is no way," grunted Helm. There was satisfaction in his voice. "No way out, for you and your insane friend, Pendragon. This passage leads only to another door in the corridor, above the stairs. The way down is exactly the same as the way up; through the gaming room, and down into the hallway. As I warned you, Pendragon, you are already dead men."

* * *

Pendragon pushed Helm ahead of them until they reached a

second door in the passage. He ordered the man to stand to one side, and Prince Albert pressed one of the heavy pistols against Helm's temple. There was no need for him to voice any threat, his eyes were enough warning. Pendragon unbolted the door and drew it inwards. As Helm had said, it led directly on to the landing at the head of the staircase. Voices shouted in the corridor somewhere to the left, in the direction of the room.

"Our only chance is to run for it! We can hold them off in the narrow passage above the kitchen; there's no chance here." Pendragon glanced out into the corridor. There was a commotion outside the far door where the men had just succeeded in entering the room and were surveying the bloody scene inside. "Go now, Sir. Leave Helm for me to deal with."

Prince Albert glared at Pendragon as though he had cursed him. "Leave Helm to you, Captain? That I will certainly not do. This man has the spineless effrontery to threaten myself and perhaps my family with assassination; tortures those whom I hold most precious. Leave him, Sir? I will not!" It was a dangerous outburst. Helm's eyes widened in astonishment. He stared at Prince Albert. His belated recognition of the Prince was obvious. Pendragon brought up his pistol to kill the man, but the Prince knocked it aside. "That is an order, Captain Pendragon. He comes with us." The Prince grasped Helm's clothing and dragged him out to the stairs.

There was a shout of warning along the corridor. Pendragon dived through the doorway in an attempt to place himself between the Prince and the men. He landed on his hands and knees against the banisters. The men were running towards them along the corridor. The leader, the foreign-looking croupier, paused to aim a pistol at them. Pendragon squeezed the trigger on the Director's small revolver, praying it was well primed and loaded. The weapon fired with barely a recoil. It was a light load and a small bullet; intended as a saloon gun for use at close quarters rather than in a running fight. The bullet hit the croupier high on his chest, making the man stumble, but failing to knock him over. He was less than eight yards away, and raising his own pistol again, now he had recovered. Pendragon fired a second time, aiming at the man's face. The man screamed and fell. The others hesitated momentarily and Pendragon took the opportunity to run down the flight of stairs to the gaming room. It was almost deserted now, apart from the card players still at their game in the farthest corner. At the bottom of the stairs Pendragon stopped again. A man shouted and dived from above, crashing with him to the ground. He rolled aside, the man's hands grasping at him. He pressed the light pistol against the man's body, and shot him through the stomach. The man writhed backwards to lie against the corner of the wall groaning.

Pendragon struggled to his feet to find another assailant standing above him on the stairs, swinging a heavy and ornately gilded chair at his head. He dodged the blow, wildly. There was the sound of a shot from below him and the man with the chair cartwheeled backwards over the banister railings to thud on the marble floor beneath.

Prince Albert was shouting, encouraging Pendragon to follow him. He stood halfway down the next flight of stairs, a smoking pistol in one hand and Helm clutched in the other. He looked more like a pirate than the Royal husband. Pendragon leapt the stairs to join him as the Prince jammed the empty pistol back into his waistband and replaced it with the other.

They reached the ground floor.

"Which way?"

"To the right . . . down towards the kitchens." Pendragon took the lower stairs in a single jump. He kicked at the carpet. It slid aside. "The hatch! Keep guard at the stairs. Here . . ." He tossed Prince Albert the small pistol. "By the count, there should yet be two shots in the cylinder." The Prince let go of Helm and caught the weapon. Helm slumped against the wall and Prince Albert rammed the large cavalry pistol into his stomach, while holding the lighter weapon pointing up the narrow scullery stairs.

The hatch was bolted by a strip of brass let into the woodwork. Pendragon, his hands sweating, fought to get a grip with his fingernails on the narrow piece of metal. He worked it sideways until it was free and pulled back the hatch. It was dark below.

He called. "Georgina."

A face appeared, pale in the darkness.

"Out you come." Pendragon reached downwards to take hold of her outstretched hands. He pulled her upwards, gently. She was covered with dust from the cellar, her hair uncombed and ruffled.

She said simply, "John." For a moment she swayed unsteadily, but composed herself. "You are safe, John, and I knew you would come for me."

"Your hand?"

She held it out towards him. There was a slight scar above the knuckle of her finger. "Nothing!"

"Come on," urged Pendragon. "There's no time." He saw her looking towards Prince Albert who stood with his back towards them. "A friend," he assured her. He swung his arm around her shoulders, gathering her close to him, and hurried her into the kitchens. The man Pendragon had struck with the pistol butt was struggling furiously beneath the table, kicking with his bound legs. Pendragon ignored him, although Georgina put her hand to her mouth, frightened. Pendragon called to the Prince. "I have her . . . Georgina's safe."

There were running footsteps at the head of the narrow staircase, and a shot from the light pistol. Someone yelped in pain. A second later Prince Albert, still dragging Helm, was beside them in the darkness of the kitchen. Pendragon hurried across to the door below the area and thrust it open. The night air was cold in his face, as refreshing as iced wine. There was no movement on the street above. If there were any of Helm's thugs still active, they thought it wise to stop their chase within the walls of the brothel.

Pendragon ran up the basement steps. The street was almost empty. A single Hansom cab remained at its post farther along the road. Near it, still tethered, were Pendragon's and the Prince's horses.

Pendragon began to walk Georgina towards the cab. There was the clatter of steel shod hooves and two horsemen charged down the street towards him. There was the glint of metal in the light of the gaslamps. Pendragon, unarmed, looked for a weapon to protect Georgina and pushed her behind him against the railings. The Prince was still on the basement steps, dragging Helm up them by sheer brute strength.

One of the horsemen shouted. "Captain . . . Captain Pendragon, Sir."

"Cox!" Pendragon smiled.

"It's us," shouted another voice as the two horsemen pulled at the animal's reins. "Beechy here, 'Dragon. By God, dash it, didn't think you'd lose me, did you?" Beauchamp's grinning face, broad as a harvest moon, grinned down at them. "Drat me, you've got the lady! I say, Cox, you see that? 'Dragon and Pr . . ."

"Be quiet, you young fool," rapped Pendragon. "Everything well, Cox?"

"Yes, Sir." Cox dismounted. He touched his flat cap. "Ma'am. Glad you're seemingly fit, Ma'am."

"I say," said Beauchamp. "I skewered some damned ruffian just outside your stables. God! Not one of your fellers, 'Dragon. Cox says his name was Gaunt or something. Dashed feller tried to shoot us. Young Ted tied him up, even though he was dead, and last we saw of him he was bouncing on the corpse's chest and threatening to spiflicate it if you weren't back safe. Blood all over the place! Macabre ideas has your young Ted, 'Dragon."

177

"That's enough, Beechy." Pendragon saw the Prince had stopped in the darkness of the area, and was watching them. "Cox, take Miss Georgina back home in that cab, will you? And guard her well."

"Yes, Captain Sir," said Cox. He slid his sabre back into its scabbard and passed Pendragon his horse's reins.

"John ..." began Georgina.

"Don't worry," he told her. "We'll be back home soon. Just another prisoner to dispose of as quickly as possible."

"I say, 'Dragon, what a hurrah, eh?"

"Come down here you ass, and stop shouting," ordered Pendragon. "Half of London will know what's happened."

Beauchamp climbed down from his horse, his sabre still in his hand. He shivered, still coatless in the dawn air, and swung his sabre blade a couple of times.

"Put that thing away. This isn't the frontier; you'll get yourself arrested. Last time hasn't been forgotten yet."

"Er, yes," grunted Beauchamp, remembering the troubles that had followed a wild charge through the streets of London's east end a year before. "I say, 'Dragon ..."

"Be quiet, Beechy, and listen to me carefully. I'm grateful for your help tonight; very grateful. But remember your promise to be silent. No boasts in the Guards and Cavalry; not a word of our companion's identity. Not even to Miss Georgina. Understand? Silence forever!"

Beauchamp was, for once, serious. "I understand, 'Dragon. By my honour, not a word ... though dash it all, Fitz would be jealous as hell."

The Hansom cab passed them. Cox touched his cap at its window.

"Ride behind them, Beechy." Pendragon slapped the man's shoulder. "Act as an extra guard. I'll see you back at Park Lane. I'll tell you what happened over a nightcap."

Beauchamp appeared happy at the suggestion and swung himself up on to his horse, to canter after the cab and drop into position some ten yards behind it. He turned and waved.

Once the coach had passed out of sight along Oxford Street Prince Albert came from the shadows, prodding Helm in front of him with the barrel of the cavalry pistol. Helm was silent and morose. Prince Albert nodded contentedly at Pendragon. "I'm glad you understand my wishes concerning Miss Georgina, Captain. For the sake of everyone connected with this matter, it is far wiser I remain known only as one of your army friends. There are complications enough."

* * *

The two horses were still tethered to the house railings eighty yards along the street. The coachman must have been true to his word and guarded them as long as he had been there, passing on the request to other cab drivers. Pendragon was grateful to the man; it was not unusual for unattended horses to go missing at night in London. They could be stolen, slaughtered, jointed and sold within a couple of hours, perhaps even eaten before the following dawn! He led Cox's horse towards the others, keeping himself a few feet behind Prince Albert and his prisoner in case Helm decided to make a run for it.

Prince Albert, taking no chances with Helm, tied the reins of one of the tethered horses to the girth of the other. He curtly ordered Helm on to the captive animal; the man mounted silently.

Pendragon climbed into his saddle, and waited until the Prince had unfastened the reins from the railings. It was good feeling a horse between his knees again, good to breathe the fresh air and to know he was still alive. It had been a long night; a long few days!

* * *

Grey streaks of dawn split the eastern sky above the city as the

179

three men reached the north section of Hyde Park, within a few hundred yards of the copse where they had met Beauchamp the previous evening. The park was deserted. The light mist had lifted but the leaves of the beech and elm trees dripped, and a heavy dew lay across the park frosting the grass.

All that remained now was to dispose of Helm, and as Prince Albert was coldly insistent about keeping the prisoner close to him, Pendragon was of the opinion the Prince planned to take the man directly to the Knightsbridge Guards Barracks, where he could be thrown into a cell until his trial. It was not, Pendragon believed, a wise move. Unless the trial was held behind locked doors Helm, now he was aware of the Prince's identity, was certain to make the most of the fact. Pendragon could see no way in which the Prince could keep his involvement a secret; there would certainly be trouble within the Royal household once his former attachment to Georgina became public news. It would be the subject of gossip and unkind speculation in every household of the country.

Helm confirmed Pendragon's misgivings. "I suppose you think this matter ended, Captain Pendragon? You forget Cragg and his leopards! Cragg is a determined man and will certainly revenge my capture."

"Cragg is dead, as are his pets."

Helm was silent for a few more minutes. "But not Von Oberstein, Captain. He is no longer in England."

"You are becoming boring," Pendragon warned. "Von Oberstein will not survive to do us more harm. Herr Stieber of the German Intelligence will see to that. A message informing him of Von Oberstein's departure will assure the German agents eagerly awaiting his arrival in France."

"And what of me, Captain Pendragon. Am I to be afforded the silken rope?" Helm laughed, wryly. "No doubt I will be tried fairly, according to the customs of this country, by my peers. I will make it quite an occasion for you, Pendragon, I promise; for your Miss Carr, also. The daily rags will suck on the story like leeches. They have a penchant for filth. No doubt I can provide them with a number of amusing anecdotes regarding your aunt's stay with me." Helm reeled suddenly in his saddle, struck across his face by a backhanded blow from the Prince.

"This disgusting creature will ride no farther," he growled angrily. "Pull the horses into that patch of wood."

Pendragon did so, wondering what the Prince intended. The man was obviously furious with Helm's attitude and threats. As soon as they reached the shelter of the trees, Prince Albert swung himself from his horse, and hauled his prisoner from the saddle.

"Wait . . ." Helm realised he had carried his taunts too far. "Captain Pendragon, this companion of yours, what does he intend?" It was the first time Helm had shown signs of panic.

Pendragon dropped to the ground beside the two men. He felt no sympathy for Helm. "If he intends anything, then you have brought it upon yourself."

"Captain Pendragon's companion?" Prince Albert grabbed Helm by his shoulders and twisted him around until they were face to face. "Is that what you call me, Helm? You know who I am; are you afraid to pronounce my name? Give me my title, Helm! Say it!"

Helm remained silent, but his face was now bloodless.

Prince Albert shook him until it seemed Helm's legs would collapse. "I tolerate many things. I tolerate personal insults because they are normal for people of my position. There are regrettably too many cowards who insult us, knowing we cannot reply. I also, Helm, accept the possibility of death, of assassination. It is the fashion in Europe today. What, however, I cannot and will not tolerate is the assumption that because I am a Prince, I am not a man. Attacks on my friends, insults to my ladies, bring the same reaction from me as from any other." He

181

thrust Helm away, forcing him to stagger to regain his balance. "You are loathsome, Helm, but it is my right to demand satisfaction from you. Here, and now! " There was a touch of hysteria in his voice.

Pendragon was horrified now he realised the Prince's intentions. To allow him to duel with Helm was madness. "Your Highness, this has gone far enough, Sir. Your feelings are the same as my own, but this matter is now ended for you. You have more than done your duty as both a friend and gentleman."

"Oh no, Captain." The Prince's voice was hard, edged with the same tone he had used in his insistence on joining Pendragon. "If you force me, Captain, then I will *order* you to attend my requirements, and you *will* obey. In this instance I am completely adamant." He looked at Helm again and his eyes caught the morning light with an unblinking coldness. "You will have no choice of weapons, Helm. It will be steel, in the custom of my ancestors. Pendragon, the sabres from the horses."

Pendragon hesitated. The Prince turned on him savagely. "Captain Pendragon, must I remind you yet again?"

Pendragon took a deep breath. The tension of the situation was making him sweat more heavily than the exertion of the previous night. He drew the two cavalry sabres from beneath the saddles of the horses. He paused again, hoping even now the Prince would change his mind.

"Sir..." he began.

Prince Albert held out his hand for one of the swords. His voice softened a little. "I realise your position, Captain. I am not ungrateful for all you have done, but now I am acting as a man and not a Royal prince."

There was an open patch of ground a few yards away. Prince Albert strode across to it, pulled off his coat and threw it aside. Pendragon and Helm followed him. "There are to be no exceptions to the normal rules of duelling, Captain," said the Prince. "You are aware of them?" Pendragon nodded. "Then give this creature his weapon. You may commence the matter without the customary sabre salute."

Pendragon handed the second sabre to Helm, making certain, first, that the man was standing too far away from the Prince to make a sudden thrust before the duel commenced. Such a trick would be in character for Helm.

"Gentlemen, please raise your weapons." The demand seemed incongruous. "At my command, you will begin. In the event of a wound the duel will . . ."

"There will be no stopping at one wound, Captain Pendragon," interrupted the Prince.

"Yes, Sir." Pendragon paused. "The duel will therefore be to the death." The word contained terrifying implications. "Are you ready, Gentlemen?"

Before Pendragon could give the final command, Helm moved with frightening swiftness. He leapt backwards, lowering his raised sabre, and bringing his left hand up from his side where it had been obscured beneath the tail of his topcoat. It held one of the cavalry pistols, no doubt taken from Prince Albert's waistband as the Prince had shaken Helm, in anger, a few minutes before.

Pendragon dived at him. The action seemed to divide itself into a series of jerky and slow movements, like those of pen-drawn figures on the flicked leaves of a child's exercise book. The Prince was stationary, as though Helm's final treachery had shocked him beyond comprehension. Helm was dropping to a crouching position, swinging his sabre backwards as though preparing for a blow; at the same time bringing up the heavy pistol with his left hand, to bear on the Prince's motionless figure.

Pendragon's outstretched hands caught the barrel of the pistol even as it finally steadied on its target, and Helm's finger tightened on the trigger. The weapon exploded in Pendragon's face, the blast of muzzle flame searing across his eyes and the

183

sound deafening him. The attack spun Helm around. He dropped the pistol and began swinging the sabre towards Pendragon's chest. Pendragon threw himself forward, closer to Helm's body, and trapped his sabre arm and wrist. He twisted, using all his strength, to hurl the man across his hip. Helm crashed to the ground. He drove the sabre upwards, blade sideways. Pendragon gripped the bright steel, feeling the razor edge bite deeply into his fingers. He grimaced with pain as Helm forced the weapon towards his face. He brought his knee up hard into Helm's groin. The man grunted, and for a fraction of a second, relaxed his pressure on the sword. Pendragon drove the point downwards. The blade slashed across Helm's throat. Blood spurted a yard across the grass. Helm shrieked, the sound ending abruptly in a terrible gurgling as he struggled for breath and sucked in a lungful of his own blood. The sword fell from his hands. He pressed them against his neck in a horrible effort to close the gaping wound. His body stiffened and relaxed. Helm was dead. From the time he had aimed the pistol to his death, less than six seconds had elapsed.

Pendragon felt himself lifted to his feet by powerful hands. "Captain?" He felt suddenly too exhausted to answer. He gripped his wrist tightly with his fingers, trying to stem the flow of blood from the deep wounds across his hand. Prince Albert tore off his neck scarf and wrapped it over the cuts. He was apologetic and concerned, as though Helm's death had returned him to sanity.

"It's all over," said Pendragon. "Nothing more to be done, Sir."

9

HELM'S BODY, GROTESQUELY TWISTED, lay on the bloodstained grass. He would not remain there long; there were shouts and the shrill of whistles some four hundred yards away through the trees. The shot had aroused one of the police night patrols. The sounds swept away Pendragon's lethargy. There were already figures running towards them through the edge of the thin woods.

"Mount and hurry, Sir." Pendragon swung himself into his saddle. He glanced at Helm's body. The cavalry pistol which had so nearly brought about the death of the Prince, was back in its saddle holster, but one of the sabres, its blade crimson, lay next to Helm's body; identifiable by its regimental code marks, should a police inspector care to check its origin. Pendragon dug his heels into the horse and charged towards Helm's body, leaning low from the saddle to snatch the sabre from the ground as he passed. He heaved his horse around and galloped back. The running figures were closer now. He grabbed at the reins of the third horse, then led it, at a gallop, after the Prince.

Behind them, running figures stopped; there was no chance of catching horsemen in open ground.

* * *

The men parted in Devonshire Street, Prince Albert leaning

forward in his saddle to rest, a little breathless, on his elbow. He smiled at Pendragon, sheepishly. "Perhaps I was more trouble than my assistance was worth, Captain. If that is the case, I owe you my apologies." He held out his hand and gripped Pendragon's warmly. "I certainly owe you my thanks."

Pendragon looked at Prince Albert. Had the man been recognisable as the Prince earlier, even without his moustache and sideburns, he was certainly a stranger now. His face was grimy, streaked pale where perspiration had run from his forehead. His clothing was creased and bloodstained, his shoes scuffed by the stirrups.

The Prince caught Pendragon's gaze and laughed. "I don't think I've managed to get so grubby since I was a lad; and I dare to criticise my own children, even now! Well, Captain, we part here. And what will you do now?"

"Back to Hampshire for the remainder of the harvest, Sir," said Pendragon. "Then here for the winter season; unless I'm required again."

"Business as usual for the pair of us, eh?" The Prince straightened himself until he was stiff-backed in the saddle, as though his Royal commitments were already upon him. "I shall go now to Mister Cloverly's, to beg clothes, and his silence. And I shall ask him to make the personal report to Her Majesty; I think it would be unwise for you to do so, Captain, until I have further time to cool the air." He was more formal now. He nodded his head in a manner Pendragon had seen him use in the past when acknowledging his officers during regimental inspections. "My thanks again, Captain. It has been an interesting night; interesting in many ways."

Pendragon sat for a while, watching him ride away.

* * *

Pendragon did not awaken from his rest until late that afternoon, when Cox, his normal and tidy self once more, knocked at

186

his bedroom door and announced the arrival of Page Cloverly. Pendragon dressed himself hurriedly and met Cloverly in his library.

Cloverly smiled, and then made his face angry. "John, I never know if your acquaintanceship should make me laugh or cry? I have had yet another palace interview!"

"You know everything, then. His Highness told you?"

"Yes, he explained everything to me early this morning, but I don't know how much I should believe. I think I prefer to believe none of it; it is only a terrible dream. I did, however, have the satisfaction of facing Field Marshal Sir Hubert Gowers an hour ago with a certain amount of good news. I was able to tell him that thanks to your efforts, and those of a certain Lieutenant Beauchamp, there is no longer any threat to Prince Albert's life. I also had the pleasure of informing him that all those responsible for the threat were dead. Tried by their own hands, and executed by Her Majesty's servants." Page Cloverly grinned. "That took the old devil's wind from his chest, though he had barely the grace to thank you, and said only that it was your work to act so. However, I do believe you are forgiven for the Piccadilly incident." Page Cloverly's face softened. "I owe you my deepest personal thanks, my friend. Though the quicker Georgina accepts my hand, the safer I am sure she will be."

"There are the usual matters to clear up, Page," warned Pendragon. "Beauchamp may lose his commission; he certainly lost his Commanding Officer's favourite hunter. There is a corpse in my stables, hidden well, and there was a body in the park; there is certainly another body at Helm's estate. And the ones in the brothel."

"Bodies, bodies," sighed Page Cloverly. "You leave the signs of your profession everywhere. No matter; they will never be officially coupled with either yourself or the department. Those in the brothel will already be disposed of—buried in Holy Land, no doubt. As for the horse, and the equipment lost, that I will deal with personally. Beauchamp's Colonel, Augustus Fuerte Hurse, is a member of my club. He's not as tough as he would have his young officers believe."

* * *

It was late evening, and John Pendragon faced Georgina at the dinner table. She was again as graceful and beautiful as ever; the only signs of her recent experience showed in the slight darkening beneath her eyes that her pale make-up failed to cover. The thin scar across the joint of her little finger, from Helm's knife, was barely visible. She seemed, however, puzzled. She held a single rose in her hands. It was the deepest vermilion, and around its thornless stem was looped a narrow strand of blue ribbon.

She pouted, and frowned; an attractive and feminine expression. "John, dear. Your companion? No, no, not madcap Lieutenant Beauchamp; the other gentleman?"

"Oh . . ." Pendragon paused with his soup spoon a few inches from his mouth. "Captain Jefferies of the, er . . . 17th Lancers."

"So you keep assuring me." Georgina stared beyond Pendragon, her eyes softening. "He is a well-built gentleman; I would like the opportunity to meet him. I feel I would enjoy his company as though I had known him for years. Your story of his bravery made me feel quite weak." She stopped and twisted the rose in her fingers, and looked hard at Pendragon, her small face tilted a little to one side. "John, dear. Do you know anything of roses which have blue ribbons around their stems?"

"No, Georgina." The soup spoon was still stationary, though dripping its contents back into the bowl.

"I had them sent to me, many many years ago. Red roses, with a blue ribbon around their stems, every day for almost three wonderful years. So many beautiful red roses; so many yards of blue silk ribbon. May I ask you, John, as Mister Page Cloverly denies all knowledge of this gift, and I have no idea who could

188

possibly have sent it, do you not perhaps think it might have come from your friend . . . what did you call him? Ah, yes, Captain Jefferies of the er . . . 17th Lancers, a previously unmentioned acquaintance of yours who was prepared to risk his life in saving my own though we have never met!"

Pendragon dropped his spoon. He dabbed at the lace tablecloth with his napkin and blushed. "The soup is extraordinarily hot this evening, Georgina. The kitchen is improving," he said, aware his voice was trembling.

Georgina lowered her head a little. There was a faint smile on her lips and her green eyes were moist.

Pendragon watched her. After a few moments she regained her usual composure.

"We are really neglecting our social engagements, John." She spoke, making her voice enthusiastic. "We must have a grand ball. Some occasion bright and cheerful to shake away the cobwebs. A hundred guests, and all of them our friends. An orchestra for music, and wine for laughter."

Pendragon's mind raced over the happenings of the past few days. Blood, and violence; the stinking breath of the man-eating leopards; pain, agony and death; Helm, the treacherous and sadistic killer who plotted against the realm; other faceless and nameless men whose bodies already lay rotting in hidden graves. They were all from a distant time, another place, a different existence.

F
TRE
copy 1

Trevelyan, Robert

His Highness
commands Pendragon

24489

DATE			
JUN 18 '76	JAN 29 '80		
JUN 28 '76	SEP 2 '80		
JUL 2 '76	JUL 14 '83		
JUL 15 '76	NOV 20 '85		
AUG 19 '76			
AUG 31 '76			
OCT 18 '76			
OCT 25 '76			
NOV 2 '76			
NOV 24 '76			
FEB 28 '77			
DEC 14 '79			

WITHDRAWN

24489